4·10·01
from BC

Buddha Stevens
and
Other Stories

Buddha Stevens

and

Other Stories

STEVEN HAYWARD

TORONTO

Exile Editions
2000

This edition is published by Exile Editions Limited,
20 Dale Avenue, Toronto, Ontario, Canada   M4W 1K4

Sales Distribution:
McArthur & Company
c/o Harper Collins
1995 Markham Road
Toronto, ON
M1B 5M8
toll free:
1 800 387 0117
(fax) 1 800 668 5788

Layout and Design by MICHAEL P. CALLAGHAN
Composed and Typeset at MOONS OF JUPITER, INC. (Toronto)
Cover by JONATHAN HOWELLS
Author's Photograph by JOHN REEVES

Some of these stories have previously appeared in
Writ, The Northwest Review, Crazyhorse, The Iowa Review,
The Greensboro Review, Fiddlehead, Canadian Fiction Magazine,
The University College Review, Henry Street and
Exile, The Literary Quarterly

The publisher wishes to acknowledge
the assistance toward publication of
the Canada Council and the Ontario Arts Council.

The Canada Council
Conseil des Arts du Canada

ISBN 1-55096-520-4

ACKNOWLEDGEMENTS

When writing these stories, I have had the good fortune to have been helped by a number of people, and it is a pleasure to acknowledge some of them here. Thanks to Henry Auster, Roger Greenwald, Trish Nicholson, Bob McCormack, Mike Matisko, Alex Lukashevsky, Andrew Biro, Alex Cobb, Norman Ravvin, Mark Hayward, Paul Pellizzari, Phil Provart, Theo Dragoneri, Pricilla Uppal, Barry Callaghan, Nina Callaghan, Michael Callaghan, and Mike DiFranco.

Special thanks is due to Katherine Carlstrom, who saw me through the trauma and psychic vicissitudes of becoming an author for the first time. Thanks also to my grandparents, Anne and Costanzo DiFranco, for telling me, repeatedly, the stories that I tell myself, once again, in these pages.

These stories would not have been written had it not been for the support, encouragement, and love of Linda Behme. She knows, better than anyone, how she moved and moves through these pages.

Finally, this book is dedicated to my mother, Phyllis Hayward, who got me reading, and writing, and reading my own writing in the first place.

Contents

AUGUST 7, 1921

After ten years of "Give-Away Days," the Yankees had managed to dole out a greater variety of baseball paraphernalia than any other team in the history of baseball. The first Give-Away Day was on June 3, 1918 (when 6,500 Yankee caps were given away), and the last was on September 17, 1927 (when over 80,000 pretzels shaped like Yankee logos were distributed). In between, there had been Cap Day, Bottle Opener Day, Pennant Day, Cigar Day, Pillow Day, Sock Day, Mug Day, Pretzel Day, Jersey Day, Sneaker Day, Baseball Card Day, Camera Day, Hot Dog Day, Tobacco Day, Chewing Tobacco Day, Cracker Jack Day, and Peanut Day, to name a few.

August 7, 1921, was Bat Day.

According to *The Completely Complete Book of Baseball Statistics* by Dr. Venus Guzman, there were 21,106 paying customers in Yankee Stadium that day, and 15,000 of them had been given complimentary baseball bats as they entered the stadium. This story is concerned with seven of those people. The first two are Mary and Lyman Labrow.

I know about the Labrows thanks to an article published on September 21, 1923 (roughly two years after Bat Day), that I found in the archives of a now-defunct newspaper called the *New York Reflector.* The article described the circumstances that led to both of the Labrows being in Yankee Stadium that day, and was accompanied by a photo of the couple; in it, Mary and Lyman are smiling and wearing clothes which were already out-of-fashion in 1921. The Grand Canyon is visible in the background. Lyman Labrow was an optometrist and Mary Labrow was a seamstress. They lived in Bergen County, New Jersey, and had no children.

On August 7, 1921, Mary Labrow was sitting one row ahead of me in Yankee Stadium. She was a small, birdlike woman and was wearing a nondescript brown dress that day. She did not look at the field once during the game. Instead, she was looking at two people sitting three rows ahead of her, at a man and a woman.

The man she was looking at was her husband, Lyman Labrow. Mary had come to the game specifically to spy on him, and she could see him perfectly from where she was sitting. Lyman, however, did not see her until it was too late; until after she had noticed the same thing I had noticed, that he was not alone.

Lyman Labrow had come to the game that day with his secretary, a twenty-three-year-old woman named Jackie Hubbs. She was wearing a bright yellow dress and carried a small white purse that had a medium-sized bulge in it. She was exactly the kind of girl you look at during baseball games when there is no one at bat.

For the first three innings, no one could have guessed that Lyman Labrow and Jackie Hubbs were romantically involved, despite the fact they were sitting next to one another. They watched the game and their hands did not even touch. Jackie Hubbs' white purse sat chastely on her lap and her white fingers were folded chastely on top of it. However, it became evident during the fourth inning, when Jackie Hubbs reached into her purse and removed the medium-sized bulge, that she and Lyman Labrow were having an affair.

I suppose that today, she and Lyman Labrow could have complicated sexual intercourse in the stands behind third base, and no one would think, or say, anything. But those were different times. On August 7, 1921, Jackie Hubbs caused a sensation in Yankee Stadium by eating a medium-sized Granny Smith apple.

She shined the apple by rubbing it extensively and energetically against her bright yellow dress. Instead of biting into it, she licked it three times, extraordinarily slowly, and handed it to Lyman Labrow. He looked at the apple, took a bite, and gave it back to her. Jackie Hubbs stroked the white part of the apple with her finger, and then touched Lymnan Labrow's lips, softly.

And Mary Labrow sat perfectly still, three rows behind them, watching.

Those are the first three people who matter in this story.

The fourth person who matters in this story is a drunken off-duty policeman from Evansville, Indiana, named John Seidl, and the fifth person who matters in this story is a sober Yiddish typewriter salesman from New York City named Norman Flax. John Seidl was sitting in the seat to my right and Norman Flax was sitting directly in front of me.

I know that Norman Flax was a Yiddish typewriter salesman from New York City because he stood up in the bottom of the second inning and introduced himself to a rabbi who was sitting behind me. Norman's mother was sitting beside him, and it was she who pointed out the rabbi to her son. Clearly, Norman Flax was the sort of salesman who was always on the lookout for rabbis.

"I'm Norman Flax," he said, reaching over my head to shake the rabbi's hand. "If you need a Yiddish typewriter, you know who to call."

"I've already got a typewriter," said the rabbi. "What should I need another one for?"

"Maybe you don't need one now," said Norman Flax. "But you never know. When you do need one, call this number and ask for Flax."

And I know that John Seidl was a drunken off-duty policeman from Evansville, Indiana, because he spent most of the game talking loudly to another drunken off-duty policeman from Evansville, Indiana, whose name I never found out.

"I gotta take a leak," announced John Seidl, in the bottom of the fourth inning (just as Jackie Hubbs was reaching for the medium-sized bulge in her purse). "And when John Seidl has to take a leak, John Seidl has to take a leak."

John Seidl was the sort of man who habitually refers to himself in the third person, and that is why I happen to know his name.

"Whattya want me to do?" asked the other off-duty policeman from Evansville, Indiana.

"Ahh," replied John Seidl, as he was standing up. "You're hilarious."

Now: John Seidl was a big man, and when he stood up to make his way out into the aisle, he steadied himself by putting his hand on the shoulder of the person sitting next to him, and almost fell down. It was not a shoulder that provided much support, because it was the shoulder of a ten-year-old boy.

It was my shoulder. That was me. I was sitting beside the sixth person who matters in this story.

Unlike the majority of people in the stands behind third base that day, the sixth person who matters in this story was concentrating on the game. His real name was Giovanni Spadafina, but everyone — even my mother — called him Sampson Spadafina. He was my father.

My father worked at the Heinzman Piano Factory where he was one of twenty-three men responsible for the manufacture of the tiny hammers that strike the strings inside Heinzman pianos. He had come to New York from Italy in 1911 with my mother. "The name of the ship," he used to tell me, "was the *Santa Maria*."

This was something that he said repeatedly. Like Christopher Columbus, my father was from Genoa, and the fact that he landed at Ellis Island in a ship called the *Santa Maria* was of great symbolic importance to him. It allowed him to claim, only half-ironically, that he had arrived in the New World in the same vessel as Columbus. I am aware this is an extremely dubious, if not dangerous, claim to make in this age of political correctness, but it is one that my father — were he still alive today — would continue to make. To my father, Columbus represented everything a man should be: he was intelligent, resourceful, brave, industrious, physically strong, self-sufficient, and very, very rich.

"The Italians," my father used to say, "civilized the world."

When he was not working at the Heinzman Piano Factory he supplemented his income by gambling, and won almost every bet he ever placed. This was not because my father was particularly lucky, but because he always bet on the same thing: himself. He had developed a routine that would usually result in someone agreeing to bet against him. First, he would walk into a bar and order a drink. Then he would begin to talk. He always said the same thing.

"In the Old Country," he would say, "everyone was afraid of me."

Then he would tell the story of his impossible strength, about the earthquake that shook Italy in the spring of 1887, and how the roof of his parents' house landed on his father's legs. He was only a child then, and said he didn't give much thought to what he'd done until after he'd done it. He just lifted the roof off his father.

"And that," he would say, "was when they started calling me Sampson."

The routine usually worked. After he finished telling the story of his impossible strength, the other men in the bar would begin to look at him, to size him up.

The truth is that my father was not a physically imposing man. He was less than five feet tall and did not look strong. There was almost always someone willing to wager he wasn't strong at all.

There were a number of stunts he could perform to demonstrate his impossible strength, and these stunts were usually the subject of the bets he would place. He could pick up tables with his teeth, perform one-arm chin-ups with another man clinging to his back, arm-wrestle three people at once, rip telephone books in half, and on one occasion, I saw him juggle a rusted cannonball, a butcher's knife, and a small St. Bernard.

But my father had to be careful never to go into the same bar too many times. Otherwise people would challenge him to do something that was really impossible. This was what almost happened when he won the tickets to the Yankees game.

I was with him that day. My mother had sent us down to East 88th Street, to the Columbus Bakery, to buy a loaf of bread. On the way he stopped into a bar called O'Malley's and ordered a drink. Then he began to talk.

"In the Old Country," he said, "everybody was afraid of me..."

I suppose that if he had been paying closer attention, he would have seen the look on the bartender's face, how he whispered to another man behind the bar, and the way they both laughed. My father would have known it was a set-up.

"All right, Sampson," said the bartender, "I've got a pair of Yankee tickets right here that say you can't lift the man sitting at the back of the bar."

"That's all?" he asked.

"That's all," said the bartender. "You just lift him up, and you walk out of here with the tickets, if not, then you pay me for the tickets and I keep them."

"*Adesso*," said my father, waving both his hands. In Genoese dialect this is an expression that can mean almost anything. It can be a confirmation, a contradiction, a compliment, a protest, a warning, a congratulation, a shout of dismay, or a way of asking someone to pass the pasta. In that particular context, it was the Genoese equivalent of my father announcing that he was ready to demonstrate his impossible strength.

Everyone followed the bartender to the back of the bar.

It was impossible not to recognize the man my father was required to lift. He was perhaps the most easily identifiable person in the whole of New York. He had been interviewed by every major newspaper, been photographed by the *Guinness Book of World Records*, and had shaken Charlie Chaplin's hand. People came from all over the world to catch a glimpse of him, or to have their photograph taken while sitting on his lap. However, many people declined such a photo opportunity because the man charged a nickel (which in those days was a lot of money) for the privilege. He had a concession at the foot of the Statue of Liberty and it was rumoured that he made a pretty fair living. His real name was Brian Flanagan, but everyone called him what the papers called him: The Fattest Man in New York City.

He was sitting at the back of the bar in a reinforced steel chair which had been specially constructed to bear his weight. He looked like he had been born in that chair.

When my father saw The Fattest Man in New York City he looked worried. He wiped his hands on his pants. This meant that his palms were sweating. I knew this was a bad sign. My father had palms that never sweated.

"I've made a bet," he whispered to me. "I have to try."

"Good luck," said The Fattest Man in New York City, as my father moved closer to him. "You'll need it."

The bar became completely silent. All I could hear was the sound of my father breathing and The Fattest Man in New York City's uneven wheeze.

"I'm very fat," said The Fattest Man in New York City. "No one has ever lifted me."

"Perhaps I will be the first," said my father, moving to the man.

Now: I knew exactly what my father was thinking. He was thinking about Columbus; about being first. I remember watching my father as he paced circles around The Fattest Man in New York City and — for the first time in my life — wondering if there was something he couldn't do.

I'm not sure exactly how it happened.

"*Adesso,*" called out my father, and in a split second, with one perfectly fluid clean-and-jerk movement, it was over. He had somehow taken hold of a foot and a shoulder, and lifted the huge man over his head. The Fattest Man in New York City looked worriedly at the floor, and vomited.

My father quickly put him down, picked up the Yankee tickets, and walked out of the bar wiping off one of his coat sleeves. "Don't tell your mother about this," he said, when we were out on the street, "and I'll take you to the game tomorrow."

They were good seats, but they weren't great seats. My father didn't seem to mind. That was before television, and he had never seen a baseball game before. He had no idea what was going on.

"I understand the strikes," he said to me, "but what's a ball?"

I was about to explain when Babe Ruth came up to bat.

He is the seventh person who matters in this story.

Now: in the bottom of the ninth inning, only the core of Jackie Hubbs' Granny Smith apple remained. She held it between her lips and made a loud sucking noise that drew the attention of everyone sitting in the stands behind third base. I think even Lyman Labrow was embarrassed, although he didn't look like he was about to complain. Mary Labrow found that she could not contain herself any longer. She stood up and spoke to her husband.

This is what she said: "Lyman, you snake, I'm going to kill you."

Unlike myself, John Seidl and the other drunken off-duty policeman from Evansville, Indiana, were paying no attention to the domestic dispute occurring two rows ahead of them. They were deep in conversation. They had already discussed criminals, the criminal mind, specific criminals John Seidl had arrested, the difference between criminals in New York City and criminals in Evansville, the trouble with John Seidl's kids, the trouble with all kids, the trouble with John Seidl's wife, the trouble with having a wife at all, and then, finally, in the bottom of the ninth inning, they began to discuss the 1919 World Series, and who was responsible for fixing it.

"It's them Jews that done it," said John Seidl, loudly.

"I don't know," said the other drunken off-duty policeman from Evansville, Indiana.

"John Seidl is here to tell ya," said John Seidl. "It's them Jews."

"Ain't none of the players that were Jews," pointed out the other man.

Norman Flax turned around in his seat to see who was speaking, and then went back to watching the game.

John Seidl saw him turn around and kept talking.

"It don't matter that none of them was Jews," he said, sounding so ugly that even Norman Flax's mother turned to look at him. "It was them Jews — they're the ones with the money."

That was when Norman Flax stood up.

"Which Jews exactly?" asked Norman Flax. "Just tell me which of them Jews it was, so that I can get them."

"Siddown boy," said John Seidl. "You don't want no trouble from John Seidl."

"I'll sit down," said Norman Flax, "when you shut up."

That was when John Seidl stood up.

Babe Ruth stepped into the batter's box. The pitcher threw the first pitch. Babe Ruth took a swing, and hit a high foul ball into the stands behind third base, right where we were sitting.

If it had been any other day at Yankee Stadium nothing would have happened. It would have been a foul ball and the game would have continued.

But it was August 7, 1921.

Bat Day.

Everyone swung at exactly the same time.

Mary Labrow reached across two rows of seats and attempted to hit Lyman Labrow with her complimentary bat. Lyman saw the complimentary bat coming at him and ducked out of the way. In fact, everyone sitting in that row ducked out of the way, with the conspicuous exception of Jackie Hubbs, who, with both of her eyes closed, was preoccupied with sucking an apple core.

The complimentary bat hit her in the face, and flattened her nose completely. There was a strangely silent moment just before Jackie Hubbs began to scream, when she reached up to her nose, and found it crushed.

And Norman Flax reached for his complimentary bat and took a swing at John Seidl.

And John Seidl reached for his complimentary bat and took a swing at Norman Flax.

And both men were knocked instantaneously unconscious. They fell forward and rolled out into the aisle, in each other's arms.

And my father moved with the same unreal fluidity with which he had lifted The Fattest Man in New York City over his head. The foul ball headed right toward us, and before I knew what was happening, he had reached for his complimentary bat and jumped onto his seat.

"*Adesso*," he told me, and bent his knees slightly, and took a swing at the foul ball, and hit it right back at Babe Ruth.

The last thing I remember seeing as we walked quickly out of Yankee Stadium was Babe Ruth lying over home plate. No one knew what had happened. One moment Babe Ruth was hitting his cleats with his bat, and the next, he had collapsed into the dust.

We walked straight home and my father did not say a word. It was not until we got to our house, until he had opened the front door, that he noticed the bat was still in his hands.

"Carmella," he told my mother, "I think I killed Babe Ruth."

What happened next happened very quickly.

My mother decided that we had to do something. So, we neither waited for the papers the next day (which said that Babe Ruth was still alive), nor went to the police station (which was already filling with the casualties of Bat Day). Instead: we panicked. We packed our things and got on a train the next morning. We came to Canada.

After that, my father stopped doing impossible things. He became a quiet, ordinary carpenter who earned his living building porches and installing kitchen cabinets. People no longer called him Sampson and he never told anyone about August 7, 1921. He died when he was sixty-two years old, of prostate cancer. They sent him home after the treatment had failed. His hair had fallen out and he was completely blind.

The last picture of him was taken just before he died, at my daughter's fifth birthday party. He had already been sent home by the hospital. In the picture he is singing "Happy Birthday," but looking the wrong way as my daughter blows out the candles on her cake. On the table in front of him there are some walnuts that he has cracked open. The nuts are still in them. My father never liked eating walnuts, but loved cracking them open. He would pick up a nut and squeeze it until the shell cracked. He was the only one I ever knew who could do that with only one hand. I've tried it more times than I can count. I suppose that this is the picture that would have to go at the end of his story. Or maybe just a close-up of the walnuts.

August 7, 1921, was the first and last Bat Day in the history of baseball. One-hundred-eighty-seven people, including Babe Ruth, were injured that day. According to the article in the *New York Reflector*, the Labrows divorced and Jackie Hubbs had reconstructive surgery on her face. In the paper she was quoted as saying that she liked her new nose "better." I have no idea what happened to John Seidl and Norman Flax. The last time I saw them, they were lying with their eyes closed, in each other's arms at the end of our aisle. We stepped over them as we exited the stadium. Perhaps they lived happily ever after.

I still have the complimentary bat that my father got that day. Today it is a rotted piece of wood, and the Yankees logo on its side has faded during the years it was kept in the damp basement of my house. The truth is that if I could show it to you, you would be unimpressed. It does not look at all like a bat that might have changed the course of history.

But I still have it. I am an old man now, with grandchildren of my own, but there are days when I go into the basement just to touch it. The feel of the wood never fails to bring back that day, the day my father became afraid. I close my eyes and I can see myself standing beside him in Yankee Stadium. The game is about to begin and both of us are singing "The Star Spangled Banner." His real name was Giovanni, but everyone — even my mother — called him Sampson. I smell the grass and hear the roar of the crowd, the final note dissolving into sunshine.

BUDDHA STEVENS

It was not until I attended the University of Toronto that I became aware of the fact that there was a poet named Wallace Stevens. Like all accounting students, I was required to take a humanities course as a breadth requirement. One afternoon in the second term, the professor directed us to read a poem entitled "The Emperor of Ice Cream" by Wallace Stevens. I was very impressed. But not by the poem — by the name of the poet. It was the first time I realized the name Wallace Stevens belonged to anyone other than the boy who lived across the street from me as a child. Today he is known as Buddha Stevens, and although it is perhaps difficult to believe, there was a time when he was not famous.

My name is Paul Bunce and I am employed as an auditor by Revenue Canada. I mention these details for their own sake. As an auditor, I am a man habituated to detail, and it is detail which interests me most. My purpose in writing is to supply certain neglected details in the biography of Buddha Stevens. I will be briefly discussing the famous Melvin Henderson Incident, as well as, of course, providing an accounting of my own recently publicized involvement with Buddha Stevens.

I should perhaps begin by stating outright that I have always been skeptical about Stevens' abilities. Doubtless, he possesses a certain talent, but I hold that this talent is somewhat limited, and that belief in any of his utterances should be qualified in the extreme. The fact that I have known Stevens since we were both very young affords me a unique vantage point from which to survey his personal development. Certainly there have been — and will continue to be — those who contend I have merely a personal score to settle with him. To my detractors, I can only reiterate the fact that my skepticism towards Stevens is less a result of my past association with him, and is more symptomatic of a general, personal exactitude which I extend to all matters.

Buddha Stevens and I were born in Ballentine Hill, a small town in northern Ontario. Ballentine Hill exists mainly because Yonge Street, the longest street in the world, runs through the middle of it. Its town hall, its church, its supermarket, its high school, its post office, its laundromat, and its police station are all clustered — like boats along the edges of a great river — within a one mile radius of the famous street. This is the centre of town, and in 1976, when we were both sixteen years old, it was the centre of the world for Stevens and myself.

We lived in identical houses across the street from each other, and both attended Ballentine Hill High School. There were two different routes we could take when we walked home from school: the short and the long. The short route was the most direct, but it was unexciting. It took us past a parking lot, Reginald MacLillop Public School (which Stevens and I had both attended until we were thirteen), and a number of abandoned shacks. The long route, in favorable contrast, took us past the apartment where Bernadette MacLean lived.

When Bernadette happened to be walking home at the same time we were, Stevens and I would walk with her. But even when she was not with us, we'd usually take the long route. On those days, we would stand outside her apartment and look up at her window. We knew which window belonged to her because she had pointed it out to us on several occasions. It was on the third floor, and from the street we could see in it a large spider plant and a grey venetian blind. I have no idea what Stevens and I expected to see while looking up at her window but I doubt it was anything overtly sexual. I know I would have been content if she had peeked out from behind the blind and waved, acknowledging my chivalric presence on the sidewalk.

"I think Bernadette likes you," Stevens said to me, one afternoon while we were standing outside of her apartment. "Why don't you ask her out?"

I had been kneeling on the ground, tying my shoe, and I looked up at him with what must have been a surprised expression on my face. I had just been asking myself the same question.

"You think she likes me?" I asked him.

"I think so," Stevens told me.

"No shit?" I asked.

"No shit," he replied (I apologize for this profanity, but I am attempting to deliver as accurate an account of these events as is possible, and this was the way we spoke to one another: people were either shitheads, full of shit, or getting the shit kicked out of them).

"How do you know?"

"I just know," he said. "You should ask her out."

It may sound incredible today, when thousands of people worldwide make the most important decisions in their lives based upon a single ambiguously worded phrase uttered by Buddha Stevens, but I challenged his opinion. "If you're shitting me," I warned him, "I'll kick the shit out of you."

"No shit," he said, earnestly.

I considered the idea, then looked at him. "How should I ask her?" I said.

"The important thing," he told me, "is not to seem nervous."

Like myself, Stevens was a virgin in 1976. Our experience of sex was limited to the instruction we had received in Health Class (taught by Mr. Williams, who had transported Stevens, myself, and the other hundred boys enrolled in gym at Ballentine Hill High School out to his farm, on three separate occasions, so that we might observe the correct method of putting a condom on a horse), a package of playing cards (owned by George Furtlong), and a dog-eared paperback book entitled *Man with a Maid* (which Stevens had found in the basement of his house).

Despite this inexperience, I still wanted his advice about asking Bernadette out. Even then, Stevens possessed the ability to give one the impression that he was offering insightful counsel, regardless of what he actually said.

"But what if I am nervous?" I asked him.

"It doesn't matter how you really feel, you have to make it sound like it's no big deal," he told me. "You have to ask her with the same voice you'd ask your mother to pass the catsup."

He then proceeded to instruct me on other matters of which he thought I should be aware: how to dress (t-shirt, jeans, and running shoes — no socks), where we should go (to a movie, but not one in which there was any killing), and finally the correct method of putting my arm around her (not like I was stretching or yawning — which is the standard practice of sixteen-year-old boys — but deliberately, as if there was nothing else I would rather do).

"If you know so much about it," I said, "why don't you ask her out?"

"You know I'm not her type," he replied.

We walked away from Bernadette's apartment and I did not have to ask what Stevens meant about not being her type. Stevens was — and still is — visibly overweight. At sixteen, he was perhaps no more than ten pounds too heavy, but in Ballentine Hill, this was enough to make him The Fat Kid. Most people called him The Fat Kid when they were describing him, others when they could not remember his name, and some when they were certain he was near enough to hear. People had been calling him The Fat Kid for so long that he had come to think of himself as The Fat Kid, and at sixteen, he was simply unable to imagine that a girl could be interested in him. We were still talking about Bernadette by the time we arrived at our street. Once there, however, we stopped, because Mrs. Johnson was waving to us.

Mrs. Johnson was a friendly older woman, and for the first ten years of my life I had referred to her as Aunt Barb. Her husband had died of cancer when he was quite young, and she lived alone in the large house next to mine. She kept a beautiful rose garden in front of her house that she watched over protectively. Mrs. Johnson was also an inveterate bubble gum chewer, and in our adolescent eyes, this put her in a class all her own.

"I have something for the two of you," she said as we walked toward her. Mrs. Johnson reached into the pocket of her green gardening pants and produced, to our amazement, Fleer Funny #34.

Times have changed, but in 1976 Dubble Bubble was the only gum worth chewing. Not only did it produce superior bubbles, but each piece of gum came with a comic. These comics were called Fleer Funnies, and Stevens and I had started collecting them when we were both still in grade school. With the conspicuous exception of Fleer Funny #34, we had a complete set of them. I had mentioned this fact several times to Mrs. Johnson, who chewed almost as much gum as Stevens and I combined.

"I found it this morning," she told us. "Just after breakfast."

After thanking her profusely, we went across the street and sat on Stevens' front porch to discuss the meaning of the comic. As is the case with most of the Fleer Funnies, the meaning of Fleer Funny #34 is almost impossible to determine.

It consists of three frames. In the first frame, a bench is being painted. In the second frame, PUD (the ill-starred protagonist of every Fleer Funny) sits down on the bench and begins reading a newspaper. In the final frame, PUD is gone, but his pants remain stuck to the bench. The man who painted the bench has returned, and is looking at PUD's abandoned pants.

"What do you think it means?" Stevens asked me.

"It's about how lazy PUD is," I said. "He sits down on the wet paint, and his pants stick to the bench. Instead of trying to unstick his pants, he leaves them behind."

Stevens shook his head. As was usually the case when we were discussing Fleer Funnies, he produced an unreasonably elaborate interpretation of the comic.

"There is something evil about the painter," he said. "He's painted the bench with some super-sticky paint in order to trap unsuspecting newspaper readers like PUD. The third frame shows the painter returning to capture his prey, but PUD has left his pants behind and foiled the plans of the evil painter.

"I better go," I said. "It's almost time for dinner."

"You should call Bernadette tonight," he said.

"Don't worry."

"She'll say yes," he called after me, as I walked across the street.

That night, after dinner, I prepared to call Bernadette with the same thoroughness that has made me something of a legend at Revenue Canada. I memorized her phone number, wrote a brief outline of what I planned to say, and practised introducing myself several times (to ensure my voice would not crack). I then went downstairs and practised dialing her number without actually touching the dial on the phone. After pouring myself a glass of apple juice (in case my mouth became dry during our conversation), I made the call. I dialed the number quickly, with my eyes almost completely closed, so that I would be speaking to Bernadette before I had a chance to reconsider what I was doing. The phone rang a single time at Bernadette's house, and my mother walked into the kitchen.

"Who are you calling?" she asked.

I had already hung up the phone. "No one," I said. "I'm just thinking of calling someone."

"You can do it," she told me. "Boys have been asking girls out since the beginning of time. You will too — there are Certain Things a mother knows."

She kissed me and left the kitchen. However, I did not attempt to call Bernadette again. The anti-climax caused by my mother's untimely entrance robbed me of the courage I'd so methodically worked up, and I went upstairs to my bedroom. Since then, I have given considerable thought to the question of Certain Things. Do such things exist? Buddha Stevens has built a career on the premise that they do. Indeed, the entire Melvin Henderson Incident implies the existence of Certain Things.

Of course, most readers will already be familiar with the Melvin Henderson incident, which first brought Stevens international notoriety. It happened three years after the events which I am describing, and by that time I had stopped associating with Stevens entirely. We still lived across the street from one another, but almost never spoke. Nevertheless, we continued to attend the same high school (there being only a single high school in Ballentine Hill), and I was there, in the school cafeteria, when the frequently mythologized Melvin Henderson Incident actually occurred.

Mrs. Henderson (Melvin's mother) had collapsed in the bathtub the night before, and had been rushed to the hospital. During the night she had slipped into a coma, and the doctors were not optimistic. Melvin had come to school that day, and brought with him a small green scarf belonging to his mother. Without speaking, he placed it on the table where Stevens was eating lunch. I was sitting at the other end of the cafeteria that day, and although I had already publicly disassociated myself from Stevens, I could not help watching him. The cafeteria became suddenly quiet as everyone stopped chewing. I could feel the eyes of the school on him.

Before that afternoon, a sizable percentage of the student population knew something about the enigmatic talent of Buddha Stevens. They knew he was almost unbeatable at euchre and that he was

26

never wrong about who would win the Stanley Cup. Some had witnessed his ability to predict which questions would be on math tests. However, when Melvin Henderson asked the question that day about his mother, no one knew quite what to expect.

It is usually the practice in biographical writing for an author to identify a "turning point" in the life of his subject — the point at which a person becomes inevitably doomed, or is assured of becoming an unqualified success. Of course, such "turning points" do not really exist. They are fictions created by the biographer in order to foster the impression that the life of his subject has followed a linear progression. I will admit there are certain moments in every life that seem particularly pregnant with the future, but it is only in retrospect that such "turning points" emerge. Quite often, the moments to which people attach the greatest importance in retrospect appear relatively trivial when they are actually occuring. "Turning points" only exist in the past. Unlike people, all moments are created equal.

However, if I were asked to identify a "turning point" in the life of Buddha Stevens, I would most certainly point to that afternoon in the cafeteria of Ballentine Hill High School. It was the pivotal moment of his life. If he had said the wrong thing, Stevens would have remained in obscurity. He would have quietly taken over the operation of his father's hardware store and never left Ballentine Hill. Perhaps eventually, he would have married Doreen Crane, a slightly overweight, but not unattractive girl in our grade. He would never have been interviewed on national television, or owned a house in Forest Hill, or had his picture on the front page of the *Toronto Star* shaking the hand of Jack Nicholson. He would've been exactly like everyone else.

"What is your question?" Stevens asked Melvin that day in the cafeteria.

"It's about my mother."

Stevens closed his eyes and touched the scarf with his fingertips. He moved very quickly, and then was completely still for what seemed like a long time. The cafeteria was utterly silent. Then he looked at me. I have thought a considerable amount about that look. For a long time, I wanted to believe it was an apology.

"Mrs. Henderson will live," he said calmly, but loud enough for everyone in the cafeteria to hear him.

Less than a second after Stevens had finished speaking, the principal came on the P.A. and called Melvin Henderson up to the office. Melvin picked up the scarf and walked out of the cafeteria. The only sound was the rubber bottom of Melvin's sneakers moving across the polished floor, but everyone continued to look at Stevens, who had returned to eating his sandwich. No one spoke until Melvin Henderson ran back into the cafeteria less than a minute later and announced that his mother would live. She had been discharged from the hospital with nothing more serious than a warning from her doctor never to eat kiwi fruit again. A huge cheer went up, and the legend of Buddha Stevens was born.

Various stories began to circulate about him: Dorothy Kendall claimed he had known the name of her second cousin's boyfriend without ever meeting him. Mr. Cobb (the shop teacher) revealed that he had been consulting Stevens about lottery numbers for a considerable amount of time. Bob Watson, a notorious storyteller in the tenth grade, claimed to have seen Stevens levitate. It was also at that time that people began to call him Buddha Stevens.

I should perhaps mention it was George Furtlong who first used the name Buddha Stevens. He was describing the Melvin Henderson Incident to some grade nine girls who had not witnessed it, and the name spontaneously occurred to him. Like most people in Ballentine Hill, George Furtlong knew absolutely nothing about Buddhism. He used the name because he had recently seen a picture of the Buddha in the *Encyclopedia Britannica*. George made the connection (as he explained eventually to a reporter from *A Current Affair*) mostly because the Buddha appeared to be overweight (like Stevens), and seemed to have a connection with the supernatural (as did all things Eastern to the provincial gaze of George Furtlong). The name stuck because it combined a mysterious sound with a representational naturalism. It appealed greatly to our literal-minded, northern Ontario town.

It was only a matter of time before the television crews began to arrive. Having been informed of the circumstances under which my friendship with Stevens dissolved, several interviewers asked me to comment, but I declined. Until now, I have steadfastly refused to associate myself with the cult of Buddha Stevens, a cult which was still very much in its infancy when I was attempting to muster enough courage to ask Bernadette MacLean out.

"It's Wednesday," Stevens said, after I had told him about my mother's inconvenient entrance into the kitchen and my subsequent loss of nerve. "If you're going to ask her out for this weekend, you better do it soon."

We were standing outside Bernadette's apartment building and I was looking into her window. "I would ask her," I said, "but she might say no."

"Believe me," he said. "She will say yes."

We began to walk home. I reached into my back pocket and took out a piece of Dubble Bubble. I put the gum into my mouth and looked at the comic.

"Let me see it," he said, and I handed it to him.

It was Fleer Funny #30, one of the most common and perplexing of all the Dubble Bubble comics, a comic Stevens and I had discussed on many previous occasions. Indeed, in 1976, it

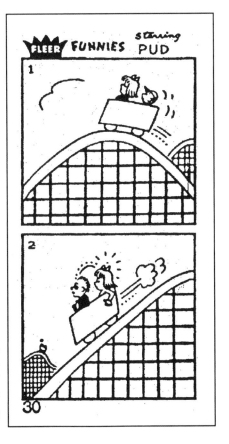

would have been difficult to find a teenager in northern Ontario who had not wondered, at least once, about the meaning of Fleer Funny #30.

In the first frame, PUD is pictured on a roller coaster, sitting behind a woman with blond hair. In the second frame, the roller coaster is in mid-descent, but the woman's hair has somehow transferred itself to PUD's head. It was the moving hair that Stevens and I always disagreed about. The explanation I proposed for the cartoon was simple: the woman was so scared that her hair had jumped off her head. The author of the comic had taken a phrase that is usually meant figuratively ("it scared the hair right off me") and represented it literally.

Stevens disagreed. He concocted a needlessly elaborate scenario to explain the moving hair. According to Stevens, the woman on the roller coaster had been undergoing treatment for cancer, which caused her hair to fall out completely. PUD takes her to the fair in an effort to cheer her up. However, his good intentions end in disaster, when the woman's wig suddenly falls off during the middle of the ride.

In short: I preferred a reasonable explanation while Stevens advocated a fantastic theory. It is this absolute disregard for rationality which distinguished him, even at an early age. Doubtless, Stevens' readings of Fleer Funnies may seem like an inconsequential detail to many readers. But it is such detail that most tellingly displays one's character. Anyone can act intelligently in a context that obviously calls for intelligence, or be heroic in a situation that demands a hero — but only a truly intelligent person displays intelligence in the smallest things. I offer my observation of Stevens' reading of Fleer Funnies not as evidence, but as detail: as an illustration of the difference between a man like myself, and one who will claim, on national television, that he knows the future. It should be plain that a person could not even consider the career that Stevens has successfully undertaken without possessing a very real capacity for indiscretion, and more than a casual disregard for everything that is reasonable.

However, when I handed Stevens Fleer Funny #30 that day, he did not debate the meaning of it with me. He looked at it, and his eyes became very far away. It was like he had fallen asleep standing up, with his eyes wide open. After a moment, he seemed to jerk himself awake. He looked at me, and it was then that I realized he had become suddenly, terribly afraid.

"You look like shit," I told him. "Are you all right?"

"I'm fine," he replied, and then after a moment, "My stomach hurts."

I tried to engage him in a discussion of Fleer Funny #30, but he seemed uninterested. He still held the comic in his hands and was staring at it, like he was seeing it for the first time.

"So," I said, after a while. "You really think I've got a chance with Bernadette?"

The question seemed to surprise him. He looked at me, and it seemed as though he was about to say something, but changed his mind. "Sure," he said finally. "You should call her tonight."

We hardly spoke for the rest of the walk home. We reached our houses and I noticed Mrs. Johnson was not outside taking care of her roses. I said goodbye to Stevens and walked up my driveway.

My parents were not at home. There was a note on the kitchen table from my mother saying that she and my father had gone shopping. I finished reading the note and realized the perfect opportunity for calling Bernadette had just presented itself. With only a minimal amount of preparation, I made a second attempt to call her. Again, the phone at her house rang a single time before I had to hang up. Someone was ringing my doorbell. I went to the door. I thought that perhaps it was Stevens, coming over to give me some last-minute advice about what to say to Bernadette.

But it was not Stevens.

It was Mrs. Johnson.

She told me my parents had been in a car accident. My father was dead and my mother was seriously injured. Mrs. Johnson said she had come to take me to the hospital to see my mother.

I pushed past her and ran across the street. Stevens was sitting on his front porch, like he was waiting for me.

"Why didn't you tell me?" I asked him.

He looked away.

"You should have said something," I told him. "If you knew, you should have said something."

He shook his head and stood up to go inside. But before he could open the door, I grabbed him by the hair and dragged him down the front steps to the driveway. I do not recall where I hit him first, but soon he was on the ground and I was kicking him.

"Please stop," he managed to say.

"You shithead," I yelled, and kicked him harder.

Mrs. Johnson came running from across the street and eventually dragged me away. She pulled me into her house and then called an ambulance. Stevens was in the hospital for two weeks. I did not visit him, despite the fact that my mother was on the same floor at the hospital, and I had to walk past his room every day. I overheard people talking about his injuries, but I did not listen very carefully. I gather they were somewhat serious.

I am not proud of the fact that I once almost killed Buddha Stevens. I am not a violent man, and I have asked myself many times what caused me to behave in such a reprehensible manner. I suppose the best — the only — explanation I can provide is that I was under extreme emotional duress and lost control of myself. I needed someone to blame, and Stevens happened to be a convenient outlet for my anger. Of course, I was not actually hitting him, but rather, the unacceptable fact that my father was dead.

I suppose many readers will regard this merely as a confession. It is certainly an admission of guilt, but I do not require absolution. I write what I write in an attempt to diminish, at least in some measure, the mystique in which Stevens has carefully cloaked himself. If his legend continues to grow at the rate it has for the past ten years, there is no telling what heights he will attain. He already seems well on his way to becoming the Edgar Cayce of the twenty-first century. Like myself, Buddha Stevens will be thirty-four this year. He is only beginning.

However, I do not wish to add my voice to the many who have already convincingly shown that Buddha Stevens' predictions lack substance. Stevens' reply to such critics is always the same: they have not interpreted his prophecies correctly. It is an ingenious and perfect defence for a soothsayer. Buddha Stevens has learned the lesson of the Fleer Funnies well. His replies never mean a single thing, and the possibility of misinterpretation is always present. As most readers are probably aware, I recently attended one of his "lectures" and saw him perform. Although I would not call it an enjoyable experience, I was actually quite impressed. Stevens would perhaps challenge my use of the word "performance" in connection with his practice, but there was something decidedly theatrical about it.

He was speaking at Convocation Hall at the University of Toronto, and although it is a large auditorium, tickets for the evening sold out within ten minutes of going on sale. I suppose Stevens would claim it was more than a coincidence that I got through to the box office with only a single phone call. It was actually a spur of the moment decision on my part. I was looking through the morning paper while eating breakfast, and I happened to see an advertisement for Buddha Stevens. I had no idea that he was going to be in Toronto, or when the tickets went on sale. Just before I left for the office I called the number listed in the paper and purchased a single ticket. It was not a decision to which I devoted a great deal of thought. I dialed the number quickly, barely even looking at the telephone.

The lecture began at eight o'clock and I arrived, as is my usual practice, fifteen minutes early. I must confess I have never seen

Convocation Hall surrounded by such a carnivalesque atmosphere. There were hot dog vendors, street musicians, an amateur fortune teller (The Magnificent Mangepanne), t-shirt salesmen (the shirts were green, and on the front of them there was a drawing of a svelte Stevens sitting cross-legged), a yellow school bus (a large contingent of senior citizens from Plattsburg, Ontario, were disembarking slowly), several homeless people asking for spare change, booksellers (selling *Seeing Is Believing*, Stevens' book containing his predictions for the twenty-first century), and a very tall man riding a unicycle while he juggled bowling pins.

I made my way through the crowd and into the building. An attendant — wearing an impressively long black robe with the words "Buddha Stevens" printed on the front of it in quite elegant, fluorescent yellow letters — directed me to my seat.

"No photographs," he warned me. "Or you're out."

I had an aisle seat, near the back of the hall and to the left of the stage. At the end of each aisle, very near the stage itself, there were a number of microphones which had been strategically placed so the audience could ask Stevens questions. The crowd was still making its way inside when the lights suddenly went down. It became very quiet in the darkness, and a spotlight suddenly switched on. It was trained on Buddha Stevens himself, sitting cross-legged in the middle of the stage, with his eyes downcast, in that characteristic posture that never ceases to remind me of a certain photograph in the *Encyclopedia Britannica*.

He had not changed much. He was older, perhaps heavier, and his curly hair was considerably more successfully managed than it had been in high school. During the show, he moved confidently across the stage speaking into a black wireless microphone, and looking directly into the eyes of his audience. He will never be a graceful man, but Stevens has managed to cultivate a rather compelling stage presence. It is not an effect produced by a single gesture, but by a certain assurance of movement; an excessive calm.

I cannot recall everything he said. He began with a series of vague pronouncements about the environment, and then made some general statements concerning the future of Quebec. He also implied that the Montreal Canadiens would not win the Stanley Cup ("unless the river comes around again"), and that the string of Blue Jays World Series victories might have come to an end ("unless the tree changes its leaves"). As always, he did not state anything explicitly.

I do not recall exactly when I stood up and made my way down the aisle toward the microphone.

While I waited for my turn, Stevens continued to answer several questions which required him to move around the theatre. He touched the hand of a young woman ("Am I pregnant?"), the baseball cap of a missing child ("Is he still alive?"), a woman's left breast ("Is it malignant?"), an earring that belonged to a dead grandmother ("Is she with Jesus?"), and made some vague statements about a younger man's lack of success in business.

"I have a single question," I said into the microphone when it was my turn to speak. "A simple question."

Stevens was at the other side of the stage, and I think he must have recognized my voice. He turned around slowly, and looked at me for what seemed like a long time before speaking.

"What do you want to know?" he asked.

"I want to know about Certain Things," I replied. "I want to know if there are Certain Things in the universe."

I am not sure what I expected him to say. It was, I know, foolish for me to think he would debate an abstruse metaphysical topic right there, in front of hundreds of his most loyal followers. I suppose I thought he would give me either a straightforwardly flippant reply, or avoid the question entirely, and that either of these would make him look foolish. However, he gave neither a glib nor an ambiguous answer. He did something I never would have guessed.

He smiled.

"I know why you're asking that question," he told me. "It has nothing to do with the future. It's about the past."

I suppose I must have nodded, because people in the audience began to whisper to each other. I was rapidly becoming another example of Buddha Stevens' remarkable powers of insight. He walked across the stage and stood next to me.

"What do you think about the Certain Things?" he said, and put his hand out to touch me. It rested heavily on my shoulder.

I leaned forward and began to speak into the microphone, but someone had shut it off.

"Was it not a Certain Thing that you would come to this place tonight and ask me this question?" he said, into his wireless microphone. "Was it not a Certain Thing ever since that afternoon when I predicted your father's death, and you didn't believe me?"

I could hear the surprised whispers of the audience. I shook Stevens' arm off my shoulder and grabbed his microphone. I removed it easily from his chubby hand, and was beginning to tell the audience the truth about what had happened, when a number of men in black robes took hold of me. They relieved me of the black microphone and dragged me toward the exit. As they carried me out, I could hear Stevens telling his audience about how we grew up together, and about how, even then, people were resentful and afraid of his abilities. I could not make out exactly what he was saying, but I recognized the tone of his voice immediately: it was the same voice with which he used to ask his mother to pass the catsup.

The attendants pushed me through the doors of Convocation Hall and left me on the sidewalk, where photographers from all the major Canadian newspapers were waiting. Three days later, the *Toronto Star* article appeared. They had interviewed — of all people — Melvin Henderson, who said that I had always hated Buddha Stevens, and once even tried to kill him. He implied that perhaps I had gone to Convocation Hall that night to make a second attempt.

Fortunately, my colleagues at Revenue Canada are intelligent enough not to believe everything they read.

I suppose that even I, at one time, believed that Buddha Stevens could know the future. I now see the absurdity of that notion, and the fact that he has used the story of my father's death to fuel his own legend sickens me. It is ridiculous for him to claim there is a disaster brewing each time he feels unwell. I have neither the time nor the inclination to catalogue the numerous occasions when he looked sick as we were walking home, and nothing ruinous occurred. It is also interesting to note that — although Stevens insisted repeatedly that we would — Bernadette MacLean and I never went on a date. After my father's death, I stopped walking past her apartment, and never again looked up at her window. I made sure I always went home by the short, most direct route.

UMBRELLA

They let you watch television in jail. I don't know why, but I always imagined there would be no television. I suppose that before I got sent here I never gave it much thought. I thought jail was the sort of thing that happened to other people. People on television. But it's not like that at all. It can happen to anyone, like waking up in the morning with a cold, or cancer. We have a television set right in our cell. It's bolted to the wall, underneath the window.

There is no antenna on the set. Instead, a thick black cord comes out of the floor and is welded into the back of the television, like a cable connection. But there's no remote control, or dial, or volume knob on the set. It comes on whether we want it to or not. We only get one channel. It's the prison authorities who decide what we get to see. Three years ago we all signed a piece of paper saying it was all right with us for them to put the televisions into our cells. It's part of an experiment in prison reform, aimed at awakening the aesthetic sensibilities of inmates. It's supposed to make us more childlike. Three years ago I remember saying this: "It's just a television, what can they do with that?" Almost everyone signed the paper.

They never let us watch anything sexual or violent. They frequently show us plays by Shakespeare, but only the comedies. I've seen *Twelfth Night* seventeen times since the experiment began. Sometimes they let us watch a hockey game, but not often. Mostly, they make us watch cartoons. In the past three years, I've watched enough cartoons to last me a lifetime. I guess that's the idea.

The cartoons we see most are the ones featuring Sylvester the Cat and Tweety Bird. Sylvester is a black and white clumsy cat with a terrible lateral lisp on the letter S, and Tweety is a resourceful yellow bird with a terrible frontal lisp on the letter T. Each episode begins and ends predictably. It begins with Tweety innocently enjoying life inside his cage somewhere, and during each episode Tweety's safety is seriously threatened by the appearance of Sylvester, who attempts to capture and eat the little bird. However, through his resourcefulness, Tweety always manages to escape. Sylvester is punished — usually brutally — at the end of each episode. They have a complicated, sexy relationship.

"Get that fucking bird" is what Dale Scott yells at the television set each time we watch a Sylvester and Tweety cartoon. He is the other man in my cell. He was formerly a professor of Sociology at the University of Toronto and knows a lot of statistics. Twelve years ago he was sentenced to one hundred and sixty-five years in prison for making movies. In the movies, he would have sex with a woman — usually a student of his — and then suffocate her. He says that he always killed the women in exactly the same way. He would put a transparent plastic bag around her head and wait for the air to run out. He did this for artistic reasons: so that he could film the expression on his victim's face more clearly. According to Dale Scott, only 22.4% of his victims looked surprised when they died.

He is not an easy man to live with. There are deep scars on both of his hands where the women scratched him while trying to pry away his fingers. He has shown them to me several times. You can't help but talk about what you did to get in here, but there are some guys who brag about their crimes. Dale Scott is one of those guys.

He is more critical of the Sylvester and Tweety Bird cartoons than I am. This is what he says about them: "It's so unrealistic — in real life Tweety would never have a chance, Sylvester would catch him 100% of the time."

"But it's just a cartoon," I tell him.

"Exactly," he says. "That's exactly what I'm saying."

My own favourite episode of the Sylvester and Tweety Bird saga involves Sylvester falling off the top of an apartment building. It happens right at the end of the episode, after Sylvester has failed — once again — to capture Tweety Bird. For some reason Sylvester is holding an umbrella when he falls off the building. During his descent, Sylvester looks right out of the television, and shrugs his shoulders. He opens the umbrella, smiles, and waves. Then he hits the pavement.

I think the way Sylvester opens the umbrella says a lot about him. It shows he is a very self-aware cat. He knows he will never get to eat Tweety Bird. He knows that he will always be falling off tall buildings. But still he opens the umbrella. It is the only dignity available to him. It is the obscure elegance of a cat about to hit the pavement.

While I am watching television I sometimes try to write about why I'm here. Dale Scott has read most of what I've written. He says that 98.8% of all criminals feel the urge to confess at one time or another, and that he would be worried if I did not feel like it. I point out to him that he does not seem to share this impulse to write.

"Sure I do," he tells me. "But I tell people, I never write anything down — you can never know whether it'll be used as part of your Offence or part of your Defence."

This is Dale Scott's criminal philosophy. It is uniquely Canadian, and is perhaps the only thing he's ever said that makes sense to me. Dale Scott says crime is like a hockey game. You commit an Offence and then you have to play Defence.

"You're crazy," he tells me. "They'll get hold of this and then you'll never get out of here."

He's probably right, but I know I have to write it down. I know that I wouldn't be able to survive in here if I didn't write something down. I know what I have to do. Like Sylvester, I'm a very self-aware cat.

This is the story.

It begins with me standing in a butcher's shop with a hockey stick in my hands.

I am looking out the big glass window at the front of the shop. On the window, the words EVANS MEATS are written in large red capital letters. It is 3:45 pm. There are people walking by on the sidewalk but there are no customers inside the shop. I don't look directly at any of the people walking by, but I can see them, and I know most of their names. Ballentine Hill is the town in which this story takes place. It is one of those towns where everybody knows everybody else.

It is not a busy street, but it is one of the main streets in the town. There was a time when my father thought himself lucky to secure such a prime location for his butcher shop. It's right near the centre of town. Down the street from the police station. Next door to the post office. Behind the IGA. Right across from the optometrist's office.

I am holding a hockey stick with both of my hands and pressing the butt of it against my front teeth. I am gripping it so tightly that the knuckles on both of my hands have turned white. I am doing this because the perfect moment of my life occurred when I was playing hockey.

I was eighteen years old and playing right wing for the Ballentine Hill Raiders. Someone passed me the puck when I was standing in front of the other team's net. The name of the other team was the Brampton Wolverines. I got control of the puck by stickhandling quickly and turned around to face the goalie.

Then I smiled.

I smiled because I knew what was going to happen next.

I put the puck into the upper right hand corner of the net. It was the only goal of the game. Everybody in the arena went wild. When the buzzer sounded to signal the end of the first period, we were winning one to nothing. The coach took me aside in the dressing room and told me there was a scout from the Toronto Maple Leafs sitting in the stands, and that he wanted to talk to me after the game was over.

Since then, the feel of the hockey stick in my hands never fails to bring back that moment to me. The feel of the goal. The calm of knowing what is going to happen next.

Even now I wish I could touch a hockey stick. But they won't let me have one in the cell. I suppose they are afraid I will use it as a weapon. I can't argue with that.

I used to keep the stick in the butcher's shop. Before I was in jail there were certain days when I would go in there just to touch it. These were days when I thought I couldn't cope. Dale Scott says that 95.6% of all people have those kinds of days on a regular basis. I am no exception.

This story begins on one of those days. The stick is in my hands, but I am not remembering how I scored that goal. Instead, I am thinking about Celia. About what I am going to say. I am telling myself to just walk in there and tell her what I think of her, and I am imagining what the look on her face will be like.

Celia is my wife. I was introduced to her by my mother. This is how it happened: we were in IGA and my mother started talking to the cashier. Celia was the cashier. They knew each other well enough to say hello. My mother shopped at IGA most of the time.

"This is my son, Malcolm," said my mother.

"Pleased to meet you," said Celia, shaking my hand.

I knew right away she recognized me. I could tell she was trying not to stare, that she was trying not to look at my teeth. After I carried my mother's groceries out to the car I went back into the supermarket and asked Celia if she wanted to go to a movie with me that Friday.

And that was the way our romance began. Like the rest of Ballentine Hill, Celia was a bit scared of me at first. She was afraid because of what happened to me in the second period of that game against the Brampton Wolverines.

It was the last hockey game I ever played. I was injured near the beginning of the second period. A defenceman from my own team took a slap shot from the blue line just as I lost my footing. The puck did more than knock out thirteen teeth. It lodged itself lengthwise in my mouth and needed to be surgically removed in the hospital.

"I've never seen anything like it," said the coach, as he knelt beside me on the ice. Then he stood up and waved to the bench for someone to bring out a stretcher.

"That puck is right the fuck in there," said Frank Fitzhenry. I remember that he looked guilty when he said that. He was the defenceman who had taken the shot. He looked at his stick like it had nothing to do with him.

I don't know what happened next. They gave me a shot of something and I felt like I was floating out of the arena. It took a while to get to the ambulance because of the photographer. A photo of my shattered mouth appeared on the front page of the *Ballentine Hill Herald* the next day. My mother didn't show me the paper until I was out of the hospital.

When I was discharged from the hospital I went back and tried to play hockey. But it was somehow different. Even I knew it. The coach told me to take my time, but soon everyone figured out that my problem didn't have anything to do with my teeth. I would stand in the corner of the rink and hope that no one passed me the puck. I thought constantly about untying my skates. That was when I stopped playing hockey.

I graduated from high school and went to work with my father at EVANS MEATS. I did my own thing. I worked during the day and watched television with my parents in the evening. On Friday and Saturday nights I would go out with my high school buddies and get drunk. But then I met Celia and I felt my life was ready to change.

We got married on July 10, 1982. I rented a huge white limousine and we drove around town after the wedding. People came out of their houses and waved to us as we passed by. Everyone knew who I was. It was a beautiful day, with hardly a cloud in the sky.

But when this story begins, my wedding day is more than ten years old. I am standing in the butcher's shop with a hockey stick in my hand and looking across the street.

At the optometrist's office.

This is because I have just found out that my wife is fucking the optometrist.

At the trial Celia insisted that the affair began innocently. I never knew anything about it. She said that it started, really, on the afternoon when she burned her eyelashes.

She was getting ready to fry some potatoes when the telephone rang. She says that she talked on the phone for less than a minute, and then went back to the stove. When she dropped the first potato into the pan, it burst into flames. She grabbed it and threw it into the sink. When I came home that night, she said she was shaken up, but not hurt.

The next day her left eye started to bother her. She told me it felt like someone was sticking a hundred little needles into it. I took her to the optometrist.

"You've got entropion of your left eye," said Dr. Patrick Morgan. "Have you been in some kind of fire?"

Celia told him about the frying pan.

"That'll do it," he said, and explained that entropion meant her eyelashes had been burned. They were curled inwards, and were slightly touching her eyeball. These were the little needles she had been feeling. "It's not a big problem," he told her. "But you'll have to come in once a week to get your eyelashes plucked."

I don't have all the details, but at the trial Celia confessed that the affair began during her third appointment. She told the jury that Dr. Patrick Morgan was plucking out her eyelashes and realized, with some embarrassment, that his hand was resting on the inside of her thigh. She didn't stop him. That was exactly the way she said it: "I didn't stop him."

They established a routine.

Dr. Patrick Morgan would tell his receptionist to call Celia and schedule an appointment. Even if she was at home when the receptionist called, Celia would let the answering machine take the call.

She would purposefully forget to erase the message, and always made sure I heard it.

"My eyelashes are growing at a phenomenal rate," she told me once.

And on the day this story begins (but before it actually begins), I found out about the affair.

It was three o'clock in the afternoon when I walked across the street to the optometrist's office. There were no customers in the butcher's shop and I put a sign in the window saying that I would be back in an hour. I'd been having trouble seeing the television clearly for some time, and earlier that day, I'd imagined that I'd seen a woman who looked very much like my wife visit the optometrist's office twice. So: I decided to get my eyes checked. I didn't call ahead for an appointment. I just walked across the street.

I was surprised to find the office completely empty. Not even the receptionist was there. The door to the examination room was closed and the only sound in the room was coming from behind it. I sat down in one of the chairs in the waiting room and pretended to be reading a magazine. I waited for five minutes. I could hear something was going on behind the closed door, but couldn't make out what either person was saying. I decided to come back at another time. I stood up and started to walk out of the office.

That was when I heard his voice. "Celiahhhhhhhh!" called out Dr. Patrick Morgan, suddenly.

I turned around and walked toward the door of the examination room. I turned the knob very gently and looked inside. I couldn't believe what I saw.

Dr. Patrick Morgan was completely naked. His hands were handcuffed behind his back. His feet were tied down with thick ropes to the bottom of the examination chair. He had a massive erection.

My wife was pulling out his chest hairs, individually.

Each time she yanked out a hair he would moan. Then Celia slapped him across the face several times. She told him that he deserved whatever he got from her. He seemed to agree. She was naked except for a pair of leather underwear. I watched for about a minute. Then I closed the door gently. I walked out of the office and back across the street. I stood behind the counter of the butcher's shop and took the hockey stick into my hands.

And that is when this story begins.

I am looking out the big glass window at the front of the shop. It is 3:45 pm. I have been standing there for half an hour, thinking about what I am going to say to Celia. I am gripping the stick so tightly that the knuckles on both of my hands have turned white.

I do not know exactly when I begin to walk across the street. There is still no one in the optometrist's office when I open the examination room door for the second time.

My wife is sitting in the examination chair.

Dr. Patrick Morgan has a pair of forceps in his right hand, and he is holding Celia's eye open with the other. They both have their clothes on, and he has just said something that made her laugh. He is plucking her eyelashes. They both turn around when I open the door. Dr. Patrick Morgan is wearing a metal headband with a light attached to the front of it, and when he turns around it shines into my eyes.

"I know," I say. "I know about you both."

"Know about what?" asks Celia.

"Don't fuck with me," I tell her.

"Just take it easy," says Dr. Patrick Morgan. "What's the problem?"

"What's the problem?" I reply. "I'll tell you what the problem is."

It is then that I realize I have nothing to say. It is like the whole thing is happening to someone else. Someone on television. I am thinking exactly that when I realize the hockey stick is still in my hands. And that is the second time in my life that I know exactly what is going to happen next.

When it is over, I walk quietly out of the office.

I can hear Celia screaming and I feel very tired as I unlock the door to the butcher's shop. The blood of Dr. Patrick Morgan blends inconspicuously into the front of my butcher's apron, only slightly fresher than the other blood on it. The stick is still in my hands. The police arrive across the street in less than a minute. We are right near the centre of town, and the police station is just down the street. There was probably a time when Dr. Patrick Morgan thought himself lucky to secure such a prime location for his office.

The policemen run into his office, and a couple of minutes later they come toward the butcher shop. They put me into the back of a squad car and take me to the police station. They send me here. They put me in a cell with Dale Scott and make me watch cartoons.

And that is the end of the story.

Dale Scott says he approves, on the whole, of what I've written. He is impressed that I haven't tried to prove my innocence. He tells me that he has just read an article about an experiment done in a prison in British Columbia, in which inmates were told to write an essay about their crimes. He says that 94.9% of those who participated tried to justify their actions. I am part of that missing 5.1%. I think that makes him nervous.

However, Dale Scott is also critical of this story. He says that it lacks closure, that too much is left hanging.

"Look at *Twelfth Night*," he tells me. "Now that's a story with closure — at the end of it everyone is married and lives happily ever after. When it's over, you really feel like it's over."

"But what about Malvolio?" I ask him. "He doesn't marry anyone."

"Malvolio is different," he replies. "He gets what he deserves."

I have only seen Celia once since the trial. I like to think that she would come to see me more often if she wasn't in the hospital. Her sickness is not life-threatening, but the doctors have no idea how to cure it. Dale Scott says that it is an extremely rare kind of mental disorder, although he admits that he doesn't know, exactly, how rare it is.

Celia's problem is that she can't stand to see other people move their hands when they talk. She will be speaking to someone, and then, quite suddenly, she will feel a compulsion to grab hold of their hands. She was sent to the hospital after she broke a bank teller's ring finger. It was an accident. Celia says she never meant to hurt the woman, and I believe her. She says she just wanted to keep the woman's hands still. I talk to Celia once a week on the telephone. She says some days are better than others.

The last time I saw her was just after the trial, before she got sick. We sat across from each other in the visitors room and tried to think of something to say.

"Yesterday," I remember telling her, "we got a television in our cell."

"That's good," she replied. "You always did like television."

And then we were silent again. We sat like that for fifteen minutes, and I know now that Celia was trying not to look at my hands, that she was trying very hard to sit still. Finally, she got up to leave.

"I'm sorry about all this," I told her. "This wasn't supposed to happen to us."

She looked at me. "I know that," she said.

Just before she left, she wiped away a tear from her left eye and I noticed that the eyelashes that Dr. Patrick Morgan had been plucking out that day had grown back. They were as long and as dark as they had ever been. Celia turned around and walked out of the visitors room without saying anything else. It was the last time I saw her.

And that really is the end of this story. From this cell, life looks less like Shakespeare and more like a Sylvester and Tweety Bird cartoon. There is always someone in a cage. There is always someone required to fall off the ledge of a tall building. There is always someone just about to hit the pavement. This story is the opening of my umbrella.

THE OBITUARY OF
PHILOMENA BEVISO

BEVISO, Philomena Rosaria — At her home
in Toronto,[1] suddenly,[2] on Thursday August
19, 1985, in her 78th year. Daughter of the
late Carmella and Paul Luciani[3] and beloved

---

[1] Philomena was making pizza dough when she felt the pain in her left arm. She
dropped the dough and tried to steady herself by gripping the kitchen counter. Then
her knees buckled and she fell to the floor. The pain spread through her chest and
she found she could not stand up. She lay on the floor and looked at the ceiling.
  "It's very dirty," she said out loud, to the empty kitchen.
  Costanzo Beviso was out in the garden and did not know what had happened
until it was too late. He walked into the kitchen carrying a large cucumber and a
basket of green beans. He dropped them both when he saw his wife. He knelt
down on the floor and listened for her breathing before calling the ambulance.
Then he went back into the kitchen and closed Philomena's eyes.

[2] Theodoro Beviso arrived at his parents' house before his mother's body was
taken away by the ambulance. It was her third heart attack and they had been
told to expect it. His father was sitting at the kitchen table and staring at the pizza
dough in his hands.
  "We knew it was coming," said Theodoro.
  "We knew," his father replied, without moving his eyes. "But not today."

[3] It had just stopped raining in the small Italian town of Montescalgosio when
Carmella DiCicco told Paulo Luciani, the carpenter's son, that she was pregnant.
Paulo did not speak for at least a minute and Carmella got ready to run. She was
afraid he had gone crazy and might try to kill her. Like all the women in Montescaligosio, Carmella was well-informed about the disastrous effect the news of child
birth could have on a man. Just three years earlier, Giovanni Mimesi (her second
cousin) went suddenly blind for two weeks after his wife informed him she was
pregnant with his fourteenth child. Carmella held her breath while Paulo looked
at the sky and did not speak.

wife of Costanzo.[4] She will be sadly missed
by her son Theodore[5] and her grandson

But Paulo Luciani had not become crazy. He was thinking that his father had warned him about such things. Paulo liked Carmella but he was not quite ready to get married. He wanted to see the rest of the world (or at least Rome, fifty miles to the north) before settling down. But then Paulo saw himself as a father and smiled at Carmella, who looked ready to defend herself.

"What do you want to name her?" he asked.

"Philomena," replied Carmella (it was her mother's name). "If it's a girl," she added.

"It'll be a girl," said Paulo.

They were married two weeks later, and although they did not approve of the marriage, Carmella's parents gave the couple a small donkey named Baroni (The Baron) as a wedding present. The baby came six months after the wedding.

[4] It was raining in Mondorio when Philomena ran into the shoe store (it had no name because it was the only shoe store in the town) and saw Costanzo for the first time. She did not know his name because she was from Montescaligosio (a town ten miles to the west) and had never been to Mondorio before. She had been sent to Mondorio by her mother to get some spices from a woman, and it began to rain as she was walking by the shoe store. Costanzo was the only one in the store that day and he was working on a very old pair of shoes belonging to a man named Rizzotto when she ran through the front door. Philomena asked him if she could wait in the store until the rain stopped, and because she had been running with a bowl of spices, she sneezed five times in rapid succession. Costanzo looked at the sneezing girl. He said she could stay in the store forever if she wanted. He was just a boy then, but he already had blue eyes that were like flashlights and Philomena blushed uncontrollably when he looked at her (but she did not make the comparison, because she had not yet seen a flashlight). He put aside his shoes, and brought out a covered plate from behind the counter. They sat in the doorway of the shoe store, eating olives and watching the rain. Costanzo asked her to marry him two years later, but Philomena had made up her mind that afternoon.

[5] Theodoro was born in the living room of a small house on Beverly Street in Toronto. It was a long labour and Philomena was certain she would die. Costanzo got home from his job at the picture frame factory during the fourth hour of contractions.

"You did this to me," Philomena screamed, when he walked through the front door. "You did this, you *gambastorte.*"

Paulo.[6] Former employee of Beviso Shoes[7] and daughter-in-law of the late Augustus

Gambastorte is the worst thing that you can call a man in the town of Montescalgosio. It means "crooked legs," and although it can refer to a man's lack of success in business, it usually means he is impotent. Costanzo, however, seemed imperturbable. He sat calmly beside his wife and held her hand for forty-one hours while she called him unimaginable names. Costanzo remembered the stories his mother had told him about his own birth. This was the way all of the babies in his family were born: they were never less than ten pounds.

[6] Paulo was born in a hospital. His mother was a thin, *mange cake* woman named Sandra Leckie whom Theodoro had met when he was in high school. Philomena disapproved of their marriage mostly because she did not believe the small girl would be able to bear Theodoro's huge children. She was only partly right, having underestimated the advances medical science had made in the thirty years since her labour in the house on Beverly Street. The thirteen-pound baby boy was delivered after only thirty hours of contractions and Sandra survived the cesarian section.

"My God," she said, when it was all over. "I'm not doing that again."

They named the child Paulo, after his great-grandfather. Paulo had red hair, like his mother, and blue eyes like his grandfather.

"Just like a flashlight," Philomena said, when she held her grandson for the first time.

[7] When she and Costanzo got off the boat at Ellis Island in 1929 Philomena already knew she was pregnant with Theodoro. They travelled to Toronto, where she had an aunt, and they moved into a small house on Beverly Street with five other families. Costanzo got a job at a picture-frame factory for eight dollars a week and Philomena had the baby. They had only been in Toronto for a year when Costanzo heard there was a shoe store for sale downtown. He took Philomena and the baby to look at it one afternoon. They spent a long time there that day, talking to Augustus Beviso, the man who owned the store. He said he was going back to Italy because his mother was dying, and Costanzo offered to run the store for him while he was gone.

Philomena was against the idea. "What about your other job?" she asked him. "What about the eight dollars a week?"

"But Philomena," he said, turning his blue eyes on her like flashlights (which she had still not yet seen). "It's shoes, and I'm a shoemaker. It could lead to great things."

The next day they went down to Beviso Shoes and — after several hours of delicate negotiations (during which Philomena threatened, no less than six times, to walk out of the store, taking her husband with her) — Costanzo signed

Beviso.[8] Resting at the Cardinal Funeral
Home (366 Bathurst at Dundas) 2–5 and 7–9
Monday and Tuesday.[9] Funeral service 3 pm,

---

a handwritten contract entitling him to eighty percent of the profit from Beviso
Shoes until Augustus Beviso returned from Italy

For the next ten years they ran the business together. Costanzo told customers he
could restore any pair of shoes, no matter how worn, to their original condition,
and Philomena began importing shoes from Italy not available anywhere else in
the city. Soon Beviso Shoes became the place to go in Toronto for Italian footwear.

But there was no news from Augustus Beviso.

It was during the eleventh year of Augustus Beviso's absence that Costanzo
told Philomena he considered himself to be the owner of Beviso Shoes.

"Be careful," Philomena told him. "You only think you own it."

It was also around that time that Costanzo began to have the nightmares. He
never talked about them, but Philomena knew when he was having one. He
would roll onto his back and say "Beviso" quite clearly, before breaking into a
cold sweat and waking up.

"You can't keep this up," Philomena said to him finally. "We have to find out
what happened to Augustus Beviso."

Philomena began to make inquiries, both in Italy and in Canada. After she
failed to find anyone named Beviso, she made an appointment with a lawyer. The
lawyer told her that the only way they could own Beviso Shoes was to be a relative of Augustus Beviso. When he heard this, Costanzo became very depressed
and could hardly sleep at all.

[8] It was Philomena who came up with the plan. The first thing she did was book
passage for her family on a boat to Italy, and take all their money out of the bank.
They closed down the shoe store and told people they were going to Italy for a
vacation. Two months later, on their way back to North America, Philomena threw
their passports, birth certificates, and her husband's driver's licence into the ocean.
When they landed at Ellis Island, Costanzo said they had been robbed and the
American government agreed to issue each of them new passports. He said their
last name was Beviso, and the immigration official had to believe him. To the American government, Costanzo was just another Italian without papers. They returned to Toronto and re-opened the shoe store. Five years later, Costanzo went
down to City Hall and said he was the son of the late Augustus Beviso. He showed
them a long letter in Italian (forged by Philomena) containing the last will and
testament of Augustus Beviso. Costanzo inherited the shoe store.

[9] Two hours after Philomena's body had been driven away in the ambulance,
Theodoro received a call from Glen J. Clattenburg, of Cardinal Funeral Homes

52

Wednesday, August 25, at St. Mary Immac-
ulate Roman Catholic Church, 10295 Yonge
Street.[10] Interment to follow at Holy Cross
Cemetery.

Ltd. Mr. Clattenburg expressed his condolences, and reminded Theodoro that there were certain practical matters regarding his mother's death that required imme-diate attention. Not wanting to disturb his father, Theodoro drove down to meet with Mr. Clattenburg alone.

Theodoro had heard horror stories about funeral directors, and as a secretary guided him through the expensively decorated funeral home, he prepared him-self to be confronted by a slick con-man who made his living by preying on the emotionally bereaved relatives of the deceased.

Theodoro was surprised to discover that Mr. Clattenburg was a short, slightly fat man who spoke very gently and slowly. He expressed his condolences again and reflected, in passing, on his own mother's death and how difficult such things always were. After agreeing on the wording of the obituary, and the times of the visitation and funeral, Mr. Clattenburg led Theodoro into the next room, and helped him choose a coffin. It took less than half an hour, and Mr. Clattenburg walked Theodoro out to his car.

"There's just one more thing," he said. "You might bring us some better clothes for your mother tonight — we have to start getting her ready."

Theodoro drove back to his parents' house. His father had fallen asleep on the couch, and the house seemed very quiet; not at all like the place where he had been a child. He went into his parents' bedroom and opened his mother's closet. All of the dresses looked very similar and he had no idea which one his mother had liked best. It suddenly seemed very important to Theodoro for her to be buried in a dress she liked. He sat down on the bed to think, and noticed the digital alarm clock he had bought for his mother as a birthday present eleven years before. The alarm had already been set for six-thirty the next morning, the time at which she had been waking up at for as long as he could remember. Theodoro switched off the alarm. It was a long time before he felt able to drive back to the funeral home.

[10] Philomena is twenty-seven years old in the black-and-white photograph that was placed on her coffin during the funeral. It was taken on Theodoro's third birthday when she realized there was only one other picture of him (taken just after he was born). She took him to the photographer's studio, and because he was offering a two-for-one special that day, she was able to get a portrait of her-self for no extra charge. Her long black hair hangs down below her shoulders, and she is wearing a plain white dress. She is looking directly into the camera, and her hands are folded neatly in her lap. Although it looks like she tried to

cover it up with some kind of makeup, there is a small love-bite visible on her neck, placed there the night before by her husband. She has only been in Canada for four years, and already she has taken over the operation of Beviso Shoes and had a son. She is learning to speak English in the evenings and it will be another twenty-four years until she sees a flashlight.

TOWER

A

The first version of this story was written on the inside of a greeting card — a greeting card that had, on its front, a picture of a bride and groom holding hands under an archway of white roses. The inside of the card was left blank, and it was in that white space that I tried to write this story for the first time. I wanted to be eloquent and brief, but also to employ a form that was properly medieval; I produced an illuminated manuscript, the kind of document on which, a thousand years ago, it would not be uncommon for a scribe to write the adventures of King Arthur.

My illuminated manuscript consisted of just one, single word: CONGRATULATIONS. I covered the Ns with red roses and gold rings. I drew an overweight cherub hanging off the top of the S. I put stained-glass windows into the sides of each of the A's, transforming both into tiny replicas of the church in which Gabriella and Professor Edward Theobald were going to be married. I extended the tops of the A's so they were banging their steeples against the sky above them, which was blue.

(The sky is always blue in medieval illuminated manuscripts. This is because blue is the colour of God; or at least it used to be, in the Middle Ages. Medieval man believed in a blue heaven: that all of the angels, the saints, and even God himself, were blue.)

It was going to be perfect, an epistle that demonstrated my goodwill while it allowed me to avoid actually *saying* anything. But, as I was colouring the sky blue, I looked at the first A, and saw it didn't look like a church at all. I saw I had extended the steeple too far.

It looked like a miniature CN Tower.

I tore the card up and threw it into the garbage. I thought I had given up trying to write this story. But then, three months later, I received a letter from Professor Edward Theobald, describing the wedding, and telling me about Gabriella's great discovery, and I sat down to write this story a second time; this time, as a story.

(That there is nothing of real insight, of profound authenticity in these introductory comments, I know. They are not here to impress. They exist as a beginning. There is a beginning to everything.)

B

I don't need to know the details. I can imagine how, and who touched who first, but I don't need confirmation.

I found out about it in Washington. In the hotel room. I went out to buy cigarettes and had got down to the hotel lobby before realizing I had forgotten my wallet. I took the elevator back up and unlocked the door without knocking.

And that was when I saw them.

Professor Edward Theobald was sitting on the bed. Gab was on her knees in front of him.

The room was completely silent, almost.

He had his eyes closed. Neither of them saw me standing there. A few minutes later Professor Edward Theobald came. She stood up to get a Kleenex from the table behind her, and that was when she saw me.

I use Professor Edward Theobald's title rather than his name because it is what he would have done. I never heard him refer to himself any other way. I have said his *title*, both out loud and inside my head, more than a thousand times. It has not worn away with use.

(As I type it now I see him bending to shake my hand for the first time. Bending was a necessity for Professor Edward Theobald. He was slightly over seven feet tall. It is a perfect height, he often told people, for a Professor of Medieval Literature — for a man who specializes in the study of dwarves and giants.)

C

I have a photograph of the three of us — Professor Edward Theobald, Gabriella Brooks, and myself — that was taken just hours before everything fell apart in that hotel room. It was taken at the Smithsonian, and the three of us are standing in front of a painting of a dead fish on a checkered tablecloth. I don't recall the name of the painting, but it must have made us laugh, and that was why the picture was taken.

In the photo Gabriella and I are twenty-seven. Professor Edward Theobald is sixty. He is holding in his hands a map of Washington and looking directly into the lens of the camera. But the flash has made him blink, and for that reason you cannot see the colour of his eyes, which are blue. His silver hair is freshly slicked back — shining with a brilliance known as Brill Cream — combed in a style that was out of style before Gabriella and I were born.

That morning I watched Professor Edward Theobald slick back his hair in the hotel room the three of us were sharing. He had just gotten out of the shower and was sitting on the bed in a grey undershirt. I remember him taking the container out of his suitcase and putting his elongated fingers into it, rubbing it into his bony hands, and then into his hair, pushing it backwards so it was flat against his skull. Then he put on his shirt. Gabriella walked over to the bed and laid her hand on his head. I love the way that feels, she said, and smiled, like she was joking.

D

My dissertation (still incomplete) was about a character named Kay, a talkative and generally annoying Knight of the Round Table. Despite his relative unimportance in the legend as a whole, he makes an appearance in every surviving story about King Arthur.

Kay is the Doubting Thomas of the Round Table. There is a moment, right at the beginning of each story, when Kay speaks up louder than all the other knights, and either recommends that they ignore the crisis at hand because it doesn't concern them, or suggests that it would be more prudent to avoid a battle because they could lose it. Kay uses different words in each story, but always says the same thing — that the adventure that is about to happen will not happen.

Kay, of course, is always wrong. The adventure always happens; if there were no adventure there would be no story. But while most critics regard Kay as an essentially dislikable and very minor character, I see him as an integral part of the legend. I argue in my dissertation that Kay's presence in the stories increases the credibility of the stories, as stories — that there has to be someone at the beginning of each story who thinks that it is not a story at all.

Kay is always that person: the only Knight of the Round Table who consistently ignores the fact that he is a character in Arthurian myth. The rest of the Knights seem to know it (whenever Sir Gawain, for example, defeats an evil knight, he always thinks about the story that will be told about the victory rather than the victory itself), but Kay is the exception. He never wants to go to war. He never wants to save any maidens. He always wants to finish his meal. He never knows he is a character in a story. Either that, or he thinks he is in an entirely different kind of story. A story about himself perhaps.

E

Medieval Literature, according to Professor Edward Theobald, is the kind of literature that no one hates to read. You always know the ending. You always know the beginning. But the beginning and the ending aren't important. What matters is the middle. The study of Medieval Literature, according to Professor Edward Theobald, is the study of the stories that everyone knows without knowing that they know them.

I met him on my second day at the University of Toronto. I was in the library, looking for the place where I was supposed to get my picture taken for my library card, but instead of finding the photographer, I found a book. I chose the book randomly, from the stacks, in the hope that the author, or perhaps even the call number, might provide me with some clue as to where I was. It was then that I noticed Professor Edward Theobald standing next to me, looking at the book in my hands. It was *The Art of Courtly Love* by Andreas Capellanus.

"An excellent choice," he said. "I recall reading it for the first time when I was about your age." I nodded."My name is Professor Edward Theobald," he continued, folding himself in two in order to shake my hand. "And you — if I might hazard a guess — are an undergraduate."

"Paul Pellazari," I told him.

And we stood there. I turned over the old book in my hands and Professor Edward Theobald stroked his beard.

(The truth is that Professor Edward Theobald was not — and is not now — a handsome man. His hair, even ten years ago, was completely grey. He had it slicked back on his head and tucked behind his ears. His beard, which was untrimmed and ungainly, was a fading shade of red. His eyelashes, which were white, were almost nonexistent, and his eyes bulged out of his head so insistently that I had trouble imagining him ever sleeping. His hands were bloodless and bony, and resembled my idea of what a dead man's hands should look like. I remember noticing his right hand particularly, because, as he looked at me, he used it to stroke his beard, as if the beard were a small furry animal that had attached itself to his face, which he was trying to tame.)

"I'm an English major," I said, and before I had finished speaking, he had snatched the timetable from my hands, considering it carefully before handing it back to me. I noticed that the paper was moist where he had touched it, and I resisted the urge to wipe it clean.

"Drop that course," he said, pointing at the Drama course I was going to take. "Instead, come to my course on Medieval Literature."

From somewhere within the folds of his huge jacket he produced a fountain pen, scribbled the information down on my timetable, and before I could say anything he was gone. His huge legs took him to the other side of the library, and out of earshot, in a matter of seconds.

I went to the first class.

There were about ten other students there. It was my first day, before I knew anyone at the University, and I remember sitting alone, near the back, watching the other students talk to each other, when the room became suddenly silent.

Professor Theobald Edward had started to speak.

He was reading a list. I discovered later that he began every year of classes by reading the same list, softly at first, but getting steadily louder until he was banging his fist on his desk and shouting.

"Jousts. Falcons. Vendettas. Malice. True Love. Ghosts. Wizards. Nefarious Knights. Magnificent Princesses" — he was getting louder — "Brave Princes. Ugly Stepmothers. Death. Revenge. Fearless Exploits. Ingenious Design. Magic. Castles. Magic Castles. Snakes. Love" — by this time he had reached full volume — "Justice. Deadly Plagues. Blessings. Giants."

I knew then that I wanted to be an English major; that I wanted to be a Professor of Medieval Literature; in short, that I wanted to be Professor Edward Theobald.

F

Fredericton not a bad place to live. I work here in the University library, a job I got through Geoffrey Booth, the President of the University, a former medievalist — a man to whom I was introduced by Professor Edward Theobald. I called him from Toronto and said that I was taking a leave of absence from the Graduate Program and moving to the east coast, and he pulled some strings. He didn't ask any questions.

(Every two months or so Geoffrey Booth and I get together in the Faculty Lounge to talk about the state of Arthurian criticism and why none of the new undergraduates take his course on the subject. Geoffrey Booth's theory is that the lack of interest in the Middle Ages is directly related to the ascendency of Beavis and Butthead.)

Most of the other librarians here tell each other that they will be working at the library for only few years. With me it is different. My visions of professorship have faded and the library has become a way of life. I have grown accustomed to a methodical existence: a life of many days but few events. I am awake by eight, at work by nine, at home by six, and asleep by twelve. I order pizza on Fridays. Sometimes I go out for a beer with my fellow librarians, but not often. I suspect working in the library has had something to do with this routine lifestyle: persistent alphabetization makes for an orderly and ordered existence.

G

Name: Gabriella Brooks
Height: 5' 5"
Born: June 4, 1964
Birthplace: Aurora, Ontario, Canada (suburb of Toronto)
Eyes: Brown
Shoe Size: Seven
Hair: Black (with red highlights)
Favourite Colour: Blue
Occupation: Astronomy Student
Favourite Things: heavy maple furniture, Marianne Faithful, aerobics, red wine, candles, playing the flute, Joni Mitchell, being kissed on the ear, terrycloth bathrobes, Vivaldi, African violets, Shetland ponies, Sean Connery, and strawberry lip gloss.

Sometimes I would call her Gabbie but most of the time it was Gab. When she was nine years old she hated her name, she said that

"Gab" sounded like the name of a goat. Professor Edward Theobald never called her anything other than Gabriella. Apparently, that now is what she insists on being called. People, as everyone knows, can be *made* by their names: call anyone a Gabriella and they become a Gabriella, call anyone a Professor Edward Theobald and they become a Professor Edward Theobald. The name is a sound that sticks.

I say her name as I type it and I notice (in a way I never noticed when I said her name every day, when it never meant anything, when I could say it to *her*) that my mouth has to become quite flexible when it is speaking her name — wide at the beginning to say the first A and then narrow at the end to complete the articulation. Gabriella. She was named, her mother told me, after an angel. Gabriella. The word remains, for me, a beautiful and mysterious sound. Even today, even after the fucking hell she put me through.

H

I have read somewhere that about eighty percent of married people who go to university marry the people they date there. Gab and I were going to be part of that eighty percent. At least that was what I thought.

We met at the University of Toronto in our first year. But it wasn't until the middle of second year that we became a couple. It happened during a party in our residence. I was drunk and she was drunk and we went back to my room. I wish the details were exceptional: that I had brushed her cheek in a certain way or whispered her name with magic results or rescued her from the clutches of a sexually frustrated leper, but it wasn't like that. We went back to my room and we both knew what would happen next. It was like saying the alphabet.

Two years after that, when we had both finished our undergraduate degrees, we realized that we had to move out of residence.

We had both applied to the Graduate Program, but didn't know if we would be accepted. We had to find somewhere to live for the summer; I wanted us to move in together.

We had talked about it before, but never seriously. Gab always seemed unsure about it being the right thing to do. It seemed like such a big step, she said, the step you take before getting married. I avoided asking her until one night when I took her out for dinner to celebrate our second anniversary of seeing each other.

We went to the restaurant atop the CN Tower; it was Gab's favourite restaurant. Whenever she had something to celebrate — the end of a school year, the beginning of a school year, a good mark on a paper — that's where she went. She had the chicken and I had the steak, and then I asked her. She said that she didn't see why not. Those were her words, exactly: "I don't see why not."

And we had nothing more to say. I looked into my coffee and Gab looked out at the city, and then she said what she always said whenever we ate dinner at the restaurant at the top of the CN Tower.

"A perfect view. The only place in Toronto where you can't see the CN Tower."

That summer we moved in together and were informed we had both been accepted into the Graduate Program at the University of Toronto: she in Astronomy and myself in English. We lived in a one-bedroom on the main floor of a house on Robert Street, my desk in the kitchen and hers in the living room. There were so many books that they had to be stacked on the floor. Her parents gave her a futon as a graduation present, and I took some old furniture from my parents' basement. We bought a coffee maker and a microwave oven and a kitchen table. And that was our home.

I

I am now thirty-one. Older than Keats was when he died. When I was an undergraduate, I thought I *was* Keats. I believed I would die young and leave behind a beautiful corpse, a handful of irreproachable poems, and a suitcase full of immaculately written love letters. As long as you are younger than Keats, you are allowed to believe that.

I once imagined that this story, or something like it, would be my perfect poem. I had visions of Gabriella unwrapping a copy of it after my death (as the proviso in my will dictated), of her sad eyes travelling across my troubled pages, of her persuading Professor Edward Theobald to give up the study of Medieval Literature and devote himself to the editing of my correspondence, and of Gabriella's subsequent withdrawal into a convent. But that's not what happened. This remains unpublished and I am still alive; the arc of my life has remained resolutely suburban.

J

J is a hook.

According to Andreas Capellanus who wrote *The Art of Courtly Love* in 1458, the word for love comes from the word for hook:

> Love gets its name (*amor*) from the word for hook (*amus*), which means "to capture" or "to be captured," for he who is in love is captured in the chains of desire and wishes to capture someone else with his hook. Just as a skilful fisherman tries to attract fishes by his bait and to capture them on his crooked hook, so the man who is a captive of love tries to attract another person by his allurements and exerts all his efforts to unite two different hearts with an intangible bond, or if they are already united he tries to keep them so forever (31).

This passage is at the beginning of the book. After he has defined love — "a certain inborn suffering derived from the sight of an excessive meditation upon the beauty of the opposite sex" — Capellanus proceeds to discuss what it means to be in love, and how to stay in love. Or more accurately, how to *keep* someone in love with you. The way to do this, apparently, is through an effective use of pick-up lines. In the pages that follow, Capellanus provides his readers with a series of dialogues between a man and a woman that illustrate the effective (or ineffective) use of a pick-up line. These pick-up lines, of course, are not supposed to be used in order to gain new lovers, but to keep the old ones (there is always *more* than one, at least in the Middle Ages).

The first time that Professor Edward Theobald met Gabriella was during my first year in the Ph.D. program. Gab and I were walking across campus one day and we happened to meet him. I made the introductions and they shook hands. I stood there and watched while Professor Edward Theobald unfolded his five skeletal fingers and saw Gabriella's hand disappear into his. And then he bent himself slowly in two, bringing her hand to his lips.

"You are a jewel," he told her.

We stood there, talking, and I noticed that he did not let go of her hand after he had kissed it. He stood there, touching her, and it looked like his fingers had somehow dug themselves into her skin.

K

Gab was, according to her Roman Catholic mother, named after an angel. But she didn't act like an angel, and she certainly didn't look like one.

She was, and still is, quite striking. With her high heels on, she is a whole head taller than I, with long black hair that hangs down below her shoulders, and blue eyes. She has a small, angular nose, and red lips that can frown with a petulance or smile with an arrogance that can only be described as queenly. Her complexion is perfect; in the six years we lived together I never saw — even in the midst of exams and the flu — her perfect skin marred by a single blemish. But really, it was her voice that made me want her most. I loved to listen to her exchange equations with fellow Astronomy students on the telephone. There was no number, no algebraic symbol, no mathematical operation which her marvellous voice could not cloak in an air of innuendo and mystery.

There had been a time, at the very beginning, when she told me everything, about each of her lovers. The first had been Ralph Moyle, he was nineteen and she was seventeen. She lost her virginity in his car while it was parked behind a bowling alley and while Led Zep-pelin played on the radio. Then Thomas Seeber, a boy in her own grade, two weeks after breaking up with Ralph (he was moving away, going to university). But she hadn't slept with Thomas, she had only sucked his dick, and he had come in her mouth. It tasted like chick peas, she told me, like hummus before you put the spices in. Then it was eighteen-year-old Joseph Franchetto, after a high-school dance when she had been drinking. She went out with Joseph Franchetto for a year; but it came to an end when people found out she had also been sleeping with a twenty-year-old mechanic named Brian Spiers, who worked in a gas station down the street from the school. Someone had seen her walk into the garage and the whole thing came out. The mechanic, she said, wasn't the smartest person in the world but he could fuck you like a gorilla — no doubt to compensate. She thought she was in love with him, and let him take her from behind. That hurt, she told me, I won't do it again.

She told me each of their names, going into the most minute detail, and I would laugh and listen in the dark while she described each of her lovers. How they touched her. How they looked when they came. I thought her absolute confidence was her way of letting me know how much I was worth, that I was more valuable than all of the rest.

We would talk about our fantasies, about the people we knew and wanted. They had to be people we knew, people from the movies or magazines didn't count. Those were the conversations that always ended with us fighting. I remember one in particular, just before everything fell apart.

"Sometimes," she said, "I think about that Professor of yours, the tall one. Look at his fingers and feet, they're so long — I wonder if the rest of him is like that."

"He's an old man," I said. "You'd kill him."

"No, I mean it," she continued. "Did you see the way he held my hand the other day, I mean there is a power to him, a kind of energy you feel whenever you touch him. He has such — presence."

"Then why don't you go live with him, if you want him so badly." I rolled over. I felt like someone had put a knife into my side.

"Are you crazy?" she said, her fingers on my shoulder. "I'm joking, it was just a joke. He's repulsive — it was disgusting the way he wouldn't let go of my hand the other day. I'm joking, come on."

"Of course you're joking," I said. "I can't believe you thought I was serious about you being serious." I lay there, staring at the ceiling like an astronomer whose telescope is a mystery to him, a telescope that is either entirely imprecise or impossibly acute, and I turned around in the bed to look at her.

L

Professor Edward Theobald's famous book is called *The Lost Lancelot: A Cultural Archetype Reexamined.* He wrote it more than thirty years ago as his dissertation at the University of Birmingham, and it remains a central text for anyone interested in the subject. After the publication of the book, he was offered a full professorship at the University of Toronto. He was only thirty-one years old — the youngest full professor in the history of any Canadian university.

The Lost Lancelot is a translation and analysis of a seventy-nine page document known now as *The Theobald Manuscript,* which is actually the earliest version of the Lancelot myth. It is a manuscript which Professor Edward Theobald discovered in the basement of a library in Birmingham when he was twenty-six years old and just beginning his Ph.D. In the introduction to *The Lost Lancelot,* he describes, in a typical melodramatic manner, how he discovered the manuscript:

I remember quite clearly my discovery of *The Theobald Manuscript* in the library that day and what I remember is, at first, that I was attracted by the colours on the page. It is an illuminated manuscript, and the illustrations are profuse — the letters are covered in red roses and gold rings, there are plump cherubs hanging off the tails of each S, and every A on the page has been made into a church with a blue sky above it. It was not until later, after I had begun to translate it, that I understood what I had found. Paleographic evidence suggests that the scribe who produced the manuscript lived in approximately 900 AD, more than two hundred years, of course, before the birth of Chretien de Troyes, whose *Le Chevalier de la Charrette* is commonly regarded as the first mention of Lancelot . . .

The Theobald Manuscript is an important discovery, because it suggests it is only in the later versions of the Arthurian legend that Lancelot is a sympathetic character — the young, handsome lover, the strongest knight of the round table who is flawed only by his illicit love for Queen Guinevere. In all of the later versions of the story, from Mallory to Mary Stewart, Lancelot ultimately achieves redemption by repentance and by triumphing over his lust.

In *The Theobald Manuscript*, Lancelot is pathetic. The poem begins with Lancelot falling in love with Guinevere, but she refuses to love him back. In response, Lancelot kidnaps her and places her in a tower, refusing to let her go until she agrees to fall in love with him. Which, of course, she does. She is then rescued by Arthur, whom she no longer loves. He puts her in his own tower, a tower designed specifically to exclude Lancelot.

And that is where the poem *almost* ends.

The final two hundred lines of *The Theobald Manuscript* describe Lancelot's return to England from the Holy Land, an old man forced to come back without the Grail. The poet describes Lancelot's armour hanging loosely around his old shoulders. His horse is standing beside him, bleeding. Lancelot is looking at the castle where Edward awaits him and the tower where Guinevere is imprisoned, and he knows that if he returns without the Grail, he will be put to death. All the same, he gets back on his horse and begins to ride. That is where *The Theobald Manuscript* ends.

M

Most people think that M is the middle letter of the alphabet. That is not the case. The truth is that there is no middle to the alphabet. The middle of the alphabet happens when no one is looking, too quickly for any letter. In the same way we say hello and we say goodbye, not really knowing the difference.

One day I went to have a meeting with Professor Edward Theobald about my dissertation. I got there early and saw the door to his office was closed. I knew he was in there because the light was on. I sat down outside the office and waited. Seconds later the door opened and Gabriella walked out.

"What are you doing here?" I asked her.

"Edward gave me a call," she said. "He's working on a paper that involves some astronomical history, and asked if I would read it."

"Edward?" I asked her.

She looked at me.

"I mean, you call him Edward."

"Of course," she said. "What do you call him?"

"How come you didn't tell me — what are you doing sneaking around?"

"I'm not sneaking around," she said. "He called me today, and I came over."

It was then that Professor Edward Theobald came into the hallway. "Children," he said, "please keep your voices down — there is learning going on, at this very minute, in these hallways."

Gabriella laughed. I didn't. She stopped.

"We can talk about this at home," said Gab.

"That's a splendid idea," said Professor Edward Theobald. "But right now we must enter the office and discuss the infinite dissertation, a dissertation about the margins of a margin."

He motioned me into his office. The two of them laughed, again.

N

While working on the article, Gab started spending a lot of time with Professor Edward Theobald. She would go to his office at least once a day, and said the article had something to do with the stars that would have been in the sky at the time of King Arthur's birth. She was never explicit, which made me suspicious, because she could have been — it was my field, after all, not hers. Gab would be co-author; it would be a major step in her career. It didn't bother me.

Which was not entirely true.

I kept thinking of the conversation we'd had that night, and I found myself walking by Professor Edward Theobald's office when I knew he wasn't expecting me, when I knew Gab was there. I never saw anything. In fact, when they noticed me lurking outside, I was always invited in. They were always civil. More than civil, really — they were kind. I began to think they felt sorry for me. I thought this had something to do with my inability to complete my dissertation and the way my academic career had been grinding to a slow halt while Gab's was taking off. I would look at Professor Edward Theobald, a serene academic presence behind his oak desk and I would think of Gab's story about cheating on poor eighteen-year-old Joseph Franchetto. She said that, each time she saw the unsuspecting Joseph after fucking that mechanic, she felt a greater love for him; or at least a genuine sympathy. And I would see Gab, looking at me with her understanding eyes, and I would worry.

I don't remember whose idea it was that I go with them to Washington; I remember Gabriella telling me about the trip, but I think it was Professor Edward Theobald who suggested that I come along, to share the driving. It was his idea.

O

"O," she said, when she saw me standing there, in the hotel room.

Round like a hole. A letter with its inside cut out. When you say it your mouth thinks it is kissing something. Or screaming. I walked over to the window and looked out and tried not to watch Professor Edward Theobald push his old penis into his pants. He didn't look at me. He stood up and left the room without a word. Gabriella came over to the window and I pushed her away. She fell against the bed and hit her face on the night table. For a moment I thought I had really hurt her. But it was only her nose that was bleeding. I picked up the box of Kleenex from the bed and handed it to her. She knocked it out of my hand, and she ran out of the room, slamming the door behind her.

"O," I said, to the empty room, looking at the used Kleenex on the floor, one of which was covered with her blood.

I packed my things and took a cab to the bus station. I came back to Toronto. That was the second last time I saw her. This chapter is about all the things you never think will happen to you even when you are having them happen, even after they have happened. Everyone, really, is the Kay in the story of his own life.

P

One of the first things I did when I got back to Toronto was have my film developed. I wasn't sure why then; but it seems plain now that I was looking for some kind of evidence, some sign I somehow missed. The film had the photo of the three of us at the Smithsonian. In that photograph I am looking at her. At the red in her black hair. I was always confounded by that redness, by how anything that black could be so red at the same time it was black. In the photo, she is looking at him — her hand is touching mine but she is looking at him.

Q

After getting back to Toronto, I tried to be an alcoholic. I went to the liquor store to stock up, and came back with so many bottles I had to take a cab home. Having bought booze made me feel better, like I was doing something real.

I started drinking. First the vodka, mixing it with tomato juice. Then I switched to rum. Straight. Pretty soon I couldn't sit up straight. I began drinking water. And then I started getting sick. It lasted for about a day and a half. I knelt in front of the toilet and swore I would never drink again, and it was during that time in the washroom that I noticed the magazine rack. I pulled out a magazine and saw it was a copy of *Cosmopolitan* that Gab had bought about a year ago.

I opened it to a page with a completed questionnaire, a number of questions which women were supposed to ask themselves before marrying their boyfriends:

1. You come from similar backgrounds.
2. He holds your hand when you're out with friends.
3. The two of you have every single interest in common.
4. You don't like the relationship he has with his mother.
5. You're the first girlfriend he hasn't cheated on.
6. You enjoy watching the way he eats with chopsticks.
7. Your early courtship was laced with coincidences.
8. Talking is rare during lovemaking.
9. You love it when his toes touch yours in bed.
10. You can't wait to get married, so you can change his bad habits.

It's the kind of thing that appears all the time in *Cosmopolitan*. But what made this questionnaire different was that in order for a girl to be sure she should marry her boyfriend she was supposed to answer half of the questions true and half of them as false. It is a level of complexity rare in the pages of *Cosmopolitan*.

The thing was: Gab had done this.

She has filled out the questionnaire exactly right: five false and five true. There was no question to who she should have married.

R

I avoided the university for a month. I called in sick and cancelled my classes. People thought I was dying. Finally Professor Edward Theobald called me. He said Gab wanted to know what would be a good time for her to come and collect her things.

"Anytime," I said. "Just let me know when she's coming and I'll make sure I'm here."

"That is precisely what I am trying to avoid," he told me. "Gabriella has asked me to inquire when you won't be there. She does not want to see you."

"That's understandable," I said. "But I think you can also see my point."

"Your point?"

"That if there is going to be any cock sucking on the premises, I will have to insist on chaperoning."

"Vulgarity doesn't become you," he told me. "And please, don't make this more difficult than it already is — no one is enjoying this."

"Come off it," I said. "I can't believe you steal her from me and then take this high moral tone."

"May I remind you — and please, don't interpret this as my taking a high moral tone — as you put it, but Gabriella *chose* me over you. No one forced her to do anything. If you think about it, you'll see that it's not really me who you are angry at, but yourself."

"It was you in that hotel room!"

"I'm not denying that," he said, slowly. He spoke calmly, in a voice I had heard before. It was his lecture voice. He was speaking like he was giving a lesson in pronunciation, like he was reading a list. "But if it had not been me," he went on, "it would have been someone else. You are not angry at me. You are angry at the world. At a world in which Gabriella Brooks no longer loves you."

For a moment I didn't know what to say. Then I asked him the question I had been asking myself since that day in the Washington hotel room: "How long?" I asked. "When did it start?"

"I don't want to be having this conversation," said Professor Edward Theobald.

"Did it begin that day when I saw you together at the office? Did you fuck her on your desk, Edward? Did she suck your dick there, while you were reading my dissertation? Did you fuck her *on* . . . "

"I don't want to be having this conversation," he said again, this time more forcefully, cutting me off. "This is precisely why Gabriella does not want to have an encounter with you when she removes her belongings from your apartment. If you are there, you will have a similar kind of outburst. And you will say things you will regret later — such an emotional confrontation will be no good for anyone."

"I think it would be good," I told him. "I think it would make me feel a lot better."

"I am hanging up the phone now," he said. "We will be over tomorrow at two. Please do not be there."

S

The next day I hid in the bushes across the street from the house and waited for them. I had to sit there for more than half an hour before they arrived.

When they did, Professor Edward Theobald was with her, and he helped her carry things out of the house. The last thing they took was her futon. It was awkward but not heavy; they manoeuvred it out to the porch and then stopped to rest. After a couple of seconds they went to pick it up again. Gab tripped and fell forward. Professor Edward Theobald was also thrown off balance. They both fell onto the futon and their heads hit. Not hard, but hard enough to surprise them both. They both laughed and I watched them kissing on the futon, his fingertips moving like bony snakes across her blouse. I wished, desperately, for it to rain. But the sun was shining and the sky was blue.

T

The CN Tower is listed in the *Guiness Book of World Records* as the tallest free-standing structure in the world. It is one thousand eight hundred twenty-two feet and one inch tall. It took thirty tons of concrete to complete. The maximum sway is three feet at the very top of its antenna. There is a restaurant at the one thousand one hundred and forty foot level. People call it the Top of Toronto. The tower has the world's longest concrete staircase with two thousand five hundred and seventy steps. Lightning strikes the tower approximately two hundred times a year. No one has ever jumped off it and killed themselves. William Eustace had parachuted out of the restaurant in 1983, survived, and was arrested immediately after. He still lives in Toronto and is employed by the Post Office. On a clear day, the CN tower is visible from a one hundred and nine mile radius.

U

These are the things Gabriella leaves behind in the apartment: one ten-inch frying pan, one spatula, one used calculator battery, one broken digital watch, seven issues of *The Planetary Report*, one issue of *Cosmopolitan*, two umbrellas (one red, one black), *Thermal Physics* (with her name, and my address, written on the inside cover in blue ink), five birthday cards (from her Uncle George, her mother, her grandmother, her best friend Julie, and from myself), two unopened packages of graph paper, an almost empty container of Secret Underarm Deodorant, seven hair elastics, two unused tampons, and a single pair of white underwear with pink roses on them and a blue bow stitched into the front.

The day after she removed her things from the apartment, I put these things in a garbage can in the middle of my kitchen, and went down to the variety store. I bought some lighter fluid.

The fire lasted less than five minutes. Then I took the blackened remains and put them in a manila envelope and walked down to the University of Toronto. I walked into University College and put them in Professor Edward Theobald's mailbox.

I think I might have gotten to the end of the hallway before I turned around and retrieved the envelope.

That u-turn is its own kind of cowardice. I took the envelope out of his mailbox and started walking home. On my way home I stopped and started walking back to the university, determined to put it into Professor Edward Theobald's hands myself; but then I changed my mind and turned around again. I did that for about an hour. Eventually I got back to my apartment with the envelope still in my hands, and dropped it into the garbage.

V

I started seeing Gabriella everywhere. Or at least I thought it was her. The first time I was walking down Bloor Street and I thought I saw her through the window of Future's Bakery. But it was only her hands. From a distance it looked like it was her, but then I went into the bakery, and saw that it was a completely different woman. Only her hands were right. I walked straight out of there.

That went on for about a month, and when I wasn't seeing her, I was seeing the CN Tower. There is no one in Toronto who does not look at the CN Tower at least once a day. Even in the middle of the night you can see it. There are two lights at the top of it that blink twenty-four hours a day as a reminder of its continued existence. I began to see the terrible thing she had done by leaving me in our apartment, in our city, alone. I was the one who had wanted to move in together, after all. I was the one who had not wanted to leave Toronto and go to a different University. Therefore I inherited both the apartment and the city, and it became a terrible thing to look out the window and see the CN Tower.

I knew I had to get out of that apartment and out of Toronto. I needed a vacation. I withdrew from the Graduate Program and packed my things. I sold my books and furniture and came here to Fredericton. It had been less than two months since our trip to Washington.

W

Not long after I moved to Fredericton, I received a letter from Professor Edward Theobald. As usual, it was typed. He prefers to type, because it is faster than writing by hand, but he will only type certain words — those he cannot abbreviate. His letter to me was in the same illogically abbreviated style that he writes everything, and its parapraxic errata brought back the terrible business one more time. I reproduce it here:

Dear Paul,

I cn only assme you stl harbor a crtn degree of resentment twds myself & my financee.

That's rht — my *financee*. Gabriella & I are going to be married and we wld like you come to the wding. Pls find enclolsed an invitation & let us know whn you will be arving. You can stay at our place if you like. There is alwys a rm for you there.

You are nvr far frm our thghts. You know from our ltrs (which you didn't write bck to!) tht we wr distrssd to hear of your withdrwl from the Graduate Program. We wish you wld cnsr rtning to cmplt your thesis. You owe it to yrself to finish what you've strtd. I suppose your withdrwl from the prgm is to be exptd. I have not tkn it personally. I mention again my offer to do my upmost to assist you should you want to return & use all of my influence to help you over any admst hurdles.

You are prbly still angry. I undst that anger. But I cnsdr where that anger is coming from. You sd I "stole" Gabriella. It pained me to hr tht, because thr was a time when you wr my friend. Whn I ws wth Gabriella I was not thinking about being your friend. Tht mch is true. I was not thinking about you. It had nothing to do with you. Thr is only G. Thr is nothing else.

Thgs are going well for G., in tht the oth ngt, she ws tking some routine slides of the ngt sky, and noticed a bright smuge in th lft hd corner of the frame. Tned out to be a comet, that only 1 oth astronomer dctmented, and sh'll gt partial credit for the discvery.

Hpe ths lttr fds you well. We hrd you are wrking in the Fredericton lbry; bt is all we know. G., as evr, snds her regards. Fnd enclosed an invitation, and plse, try to attend.
Yours,
Professor Edward Theobald

Of course, I didn't go to the wedding. But on the day it happened, I went out and bought a greeting card that had a picture of a bride and a groom on its front holding hands under an archway of white roses. It was on the inside of that card that I tried to write this story for the first time.

X

After the wedding, I decided to call her. She was living with Professor Edward Theobald so I didn't have to look up the number. I don't know what I would have done if he had picked up the phone. I supposed I was ready, poised, to hang up. But I didn't have to.

I could tell she was surprised. We talked about nothing. We talked about the weather, about the fact that the Blue Jays might win the World Series for the third time, and about her discovery of the comet. It was going to be named the Brooks-Cobb comet, because a British astronomer named Cobb had also noticed its appearance in the sky. It struck me as terribly poetic to have something in the sky named after oneself, I thought, and I told her so.

"It's not such a big deal," she told me. "When you discover a comet you don't really have to do anything — you just have to be looking in the right place at the right time. Everyone has a comet pass over them at one time or another — the trick is to notice it. My comet will be back in another five hundred and seventy-two years, they come and go."

Y

Y is a letter that needs no extrapolation. It stands for itself. Y is composed of one upward stroke of the pen that suddenly becomes two. Like one road that suddenly becomes split. There is no going straight with the Y. The Y either goes to the right or to the left. If the Y went straight it wouldn't be a Y. It would be an I. An I is a Y in which everything worked out. You need both letters in the alphabet.

Z

So what can you do? One thing: you build a tower. The tower never works. You knock down the tower. You tell a story about the tower not working. About a woman who does not stay in her tower and the tragedy that happens to her and her lover. Or: you tell a story that is itself a tower. But not a tower that keeps anyone prisoner. A story like the CN Tower, a tower in which no one can live, but everyone can see. This is the story of Professor Edward Theobald's and Gabriella Brooks's life together. The story of their falling in love. The story of their love. It is the story that lies forever and for good at the centre of their lives. I am the protagonist, the central character, the hero. They are characters in a story about me.

MY GRANDFATHER'S
BEAUTIFUL HAIR

"It's a small animal that eats the hair," my grandfather is saying to me at the kitchen table. "You can't see it, but it's there. It eats the root of the hair."

"It eats the hair?" I ask.

"That's what they say," he tells me.

"Well then," I ask, "where does the animal come from? How do people get infected by it?"

My grandfather looks confused, then angry; as if I am asking a question to which I should already know the answer. "It comes from combs — dirty combs you find on the street," he says.

I can tell that he is not completely certain about how the creature gets onto people's heads. He explains that he cannot remember all of the details concerning the animal. He read about it last week in the *Toronto Star*. He says that he thinks the animal attaches itself to discarded combs because these seem like a logical habitat for an animal that lives on hair. He agrees — when I question him further — that the weak part of this hypothesis is that it requires a great number of people to brush their hair with combs they find on the street.

"I'll find the article," he says to me, getting up from the kitchen table and walking into the laundry room where my grandparents keep the old newspapers. "You'll see."

"We're about to eat," grandmother says to him. "Find it later."

My grandfather does not reply. He pretends not to hear her, and flips angrily through last week's *Toronto Stars* for evidence of the hair-eating animal.

"See the thanks I get for making Sunday lunch?" my grandmother says to my mother. "Every day it's the same thing. I get sick and tired of it. One day I'm gonna quit cooking for good."

"Take it easy, Ma," my mother says. "Remember what the doctor said."

Baldness has always been a contentious issue in my family. The hair-eating animal is a recent addition to the arsenal of explanations my grandfather habitually keeps in reserve to explain excessive hair-loss. He attributes baldness in different people to a variety of causes, depending on their temperament, the circumstances and his own prejudices toward them. My grandfather maintains that his brother Tony's baldness is not due to the sustained efforts of an invisible hair-eating animal, but rather that Tony's hairless head is the lamentable — but inevitable — consequence of smoking cigarettes. Similarly, my grandfather maintains that his own father's lack of hair occurred because he never went to church or because he ate too much watermelon (depending on whether he wants to portray his father as irreligious or gluttonous). Even my mother has her own theory of baldness, which she expresses infrequently but clings to nonetheless.

"Your hair is like a plant," she told me once when I was seven years old and refused to remove my Blue Jays cap before entering church. "If you cover it all the time with a hat, it will die and fall out. You have to let it breathe. Just look at your grandfather."

"It's true," said my grandfather, who was in the process of removing his fedora, and was never opposed to the invention of a new explanation of hair-loss. "When I came over from the old country I had beautiful hair. But then I started working and wearing hats, and my hair fell out."

Even though I was only seven years old at the time, I had already been shown the pictures of my grandfather's beautiful hair. There are two pictures of it in existence. In the first picture my grandfather is two years old. He is sitting on his mother's knee in Montescaglioso, his home town in Italy. They both have beautiful, curly black hair. The second picture of my grandfather's beautiful hair was taken when he was twenty. He had already been in Canada for three years. He was earning a living primarily in a picture-frame factory during the week, and secondarily by selling bananas on Saturdays in Kensington market, and by shaving the beards off the other twelve men who lived in the same boarding house as him on Sunday mornings. In the picture he is sitting uncomfortably with his legs pushed to the right and his head facing to the left. It is a stiff pose. A pose designed by a photographer to seem appropriate to a man who had only had his picture taken once before in his life. My grandfather's beautiful hair is slicked straight back in a way that makes him look like Rudolf Valentino.

"It has nothing to do with small animals that eat the hair," I say to my grandfather, who is still rummaging though the papers in the laundry room. "Baldness is a matter of genetics."

My grandfather momentarily ceases looking through last week's papers and looks at me.

"The gene that causes baldness is passed matriarchically," I tell him. "It's something that's decided when you're born. You have nothing to do with it."

My grandfather looks at me sadly. Unlike most grandparents who find themselves alienated from their grandchildren by radical haircuts and unhinging music, my grandfather seems to regard gene expression for alopecia as the emblem of the generation gap. "You'll see," he tells me, and returns to last week's news.

I look at my mother for moral support.

"I'm staying out of this," she says. "When your grandfather has made up his mind, he's made up his mind."

My mother is making the salad at the kitchen counter. She sprinkles some wine vinegar onto the lettuce, tosses it and tastes it. Holding a piece of lettuce in her mouth, she sucks on it for a few seconds before she chews it up and swallows it. Then she shakes a little bit more vinegar into the bowl, tosses the salad and tastes it again. I know that the routine of sprinkling, tossing and tasting will continue until she thinks she has the ingredients mixed just right. Then she will ask my grandmother to come over and taste it.

"Hey Mom," she says finally. "Come and taste the salad."

My grandmother puts down the wooden spoon with which she had been stirring the pot of linguini, and walks slowly across the kitchen. She randomly selects a leaf from the bowl and eats it. "Perfect," she tells my mother. "No one makes a salad like my Maria."

My grandmother walks slowly back to the stove. She stirs the pot slowly for a few minutes and then slowly extracts a single strand of linguini from the pot and runs it under some cold water. When it is cold enough, she puts it into her mouth and chews it slowly.

"Perfect," she says. "*Al dente*. Take them out."

That my grandmother does everything slowly is not a choice of her own. There was a time when she did everything quickly. She has been forced to change her lifestyle.

Her heart attack happened about a year ago. My grandfather had just complained that the pasta was overcooked. My grandmother started yelling back at him: she was fed up; she was tired of him complaining; one day she was going to quit cooking for good. Suddenly, she was unable to catch her breath and collapsed face first into her plate of pasta before anyone knew what was happening. At the hospital, the doctor said that she had suffered a "subendocardial myocardial infarction" and that she would have to change her lifestyle.

"Your grandfather just left," she told me once when I came to visit her in the hospital. "He was supposed to come this morning, but he only got here a couple of hours ago."

"What took him so long?" I asked.

"He left early enough," she said. "But he had trouble on the subway. He said he wasn't sure where to get off."

Later that evening I called my grandfather. "I hear you got lost on the subway today," I told him.

"I don't get lost on the subway," he replied. "I been taking the subway longer than you been alive."

My grandmother turns off the burner and takes the pot off the stove. She motions to me to come over to the counter. I lift up the pot and pour the contents into the strainer that is sitting in the kitchen sink. As I pour out the boiling water, steam rises into my face and clouds my glasses. When the pasta is all out of the pot, I put it back on the stove.

"What a strong boy I got," my grandmother says, giving me a little pinch on the cheek. "What a good boy."

"I hope this isn't overcooked," says my grandfather as my grandmother sets the pasta down on the table. He says this because he knows it is exactly what will make my grandmother angry.

"Do you hear that?" says my grandmother, to no one in particular. "That is what I have to put up with. That is what I get for making lunch. I get sick of it. Sometimes I just get fed up. If you don't watch, I'm going to quit cooking."

"Take it easy, Ma," says my mother. "Remember what the doctor said."

Ever since the heart attack, we get worried whenever my grandmother raises her voice. The doctor at the hospital told us that the next time she falls down face first into her pasta, it will probably be for the last time. She has been told to change her lifestyle. She has been told to take her medicine regularly. She has been told to take salt out of her diet. She has been told to stop yelling. She has been told not to get excited. It is for her own good.

My grandfather tastes the first of the linguini. "Perfect," he says. "No one makes linguini like your grandmother."

"*Madonn*. . ." says my grandmother, preferring to ignore the fact that she has just received a compliment. "If you don't watch out, I'm gonna quit cooking."

They are having an old argument. It is the same argument they had last week. It is the same argument they had the week before that. It is the same argument that has been going on for as long as I can remember. It is a kind of programmed hostility that replaces the affection they must have once felt for each other. They are not really having an argument; they are just talking. They have been yelling at each other for so long they have forgotten how to do anything else. I wonder sometimes if my mother and father would interact in a similar manner if my father were still alive.

My father was killed in a car accident by a drunk driver when I was three years old. Years later my mother showed me a newspaper clipping of the accident.

"That's his car," she said, carefully unfolding the yellowed newsprint and handing it to me. "Look at the mirror on the driver's side."

I looked closely at the black and white photo of a mangled Volkswagon crumpled up against a lamp post. I could barely make out a tattered piece of cloth hanging on the mirror.

"That's your father's scarf," she told me. "He was wearing it when he went to work that morning. When I saw it in the paper it just about killed me."

After she showed me the newspaper clipping, she folded it neatly and put it back in the drawer where she got it from. She is the kind of woman who decides what needs to be done, then does it.

"What is the name of the animal that eats the hair?" I ask my grandfather.

"I don't know," he says. "I just read about it."

"What day was it in the *Star*?" my mother asks him. "Maybe I saw it too."

"I can't remember what day, but they found it in Newmarket. It was in the schools and ate all the kids' hair."

My mother explains her father's mistake. She has seen the article. In Newmarket, some children at one of the public schools became infected by a rare tropical parasite that attacks the roots of the hair and causes baldness. My mother describes the picture that accompanied the article of several kindergarten children touching their bald heads in wonder. Somehow my grandfather has got it into his head that he contracted the same parasite.

"I told you," my grandfather says to me. "I may be old, but I'm not that old. I can still tell what's what."

"You could have fooled me," says my grandmother.

"Never mind, Annie," he tells her. "You can all laugh at me if you want, but when I'm gone, you'll see that I was right about a lot of things."

"Here we go again," says my grandmother.

"What do you mean, here we go again?" my grandfather asks her.

"Do you see what I have to put up with?" she says to my mother. "This is all I get, all day, every day. Sometimes I get fed up. I just get fed up."

"Take it easy, Ma," says my mother.

"What am I gonna do?" my grandfather asks us. "Not talk about it? I can't eat, I can't sleep, I can't piss, I can't have sex — what's the use of living?"

"This is all I get," my grandmother says. "I don't even want to talk about last Wednesday. I don't want to get into that."

"What happened last Wednesday?" asks my mother and looks at them both. "Did something happen last Wednesday that you're not telling me about?"

"Nothing happened," says my grandfather.

"You call that nothing?" my grandmother asks him. "Here I am scared to death for six hours and you call it nothing."

"What happened?" asks my mother a second time.

"Nothing happened," says my grandfather, more softly. "I just forgot to call your mother."

"Where were you?" asks my mother. She is looking at him angrily. It is a look that I recognize. It is the stern look of a parent who wants to find out exactly what happened in her house while she was away.

"Go ahead then," my grandfather says. "Tell them. You want to tell them. You brought it up in the first place. Just tell them."

"Your father went out last Wednesday to buy some bananas," says my grandmother. "They were on sale at the Ferlisi Brothers for twenty-four cents, so I said go and pick up some and I'll make some banana cake. He was doing nothing, so I figured he wouldn't mind. This was at ten. When he's not back by three, I start to get worried. He gets here at five and says that he got lost."

"What happened, Dad?" asks my mother. "Did you get lost?"

"I don't get lost," replies my grandfather. "I been driving these streets since before you were born."

"Then what took you so long?" asks my grandmother.

"I got shopping at Ferlisi Brothers, and I ran into Tony DiCarnuto," explains my grandfather. "He said that his daughter is getting married and wanted to know if we wanted to come to the reception."

"Dad," says my mother, softly. "Tony DiCarnuto passed away last spring. We went to the funeral."

My grandfather looks at my mother. For a moment, he looks like he is about to say something, but he thinks better of it and only sighs instead.

"Are you forgetting things again?" asks my mother. "If you are, then it is something we have to know about."

"He forgets everything," says my grandmother. "The other day he's downstairs for three hours. I go down to see what he's doing, and he's just sitting there. When I come down, he asks me where I put the hammer. I tell him that it's where it's always been: in his tool box. I have to show him the tool box."

"You're going to have to tell Dr. Fogel about this," says my mother. She is the kind of woman who decides what needs to be done, and does it. I know that she will start watching my grandfather very closely. He will not be allowed to go out alone. He will not be allowed to drive. He will not be allowed to eat the same foods. He will need to take special medication. He will have to change his lifestyle. It will be for his own good.

We finish the meal in silence. At one point I try to tell a funny story about a student in one of my classes who went to the wrong exam, but no one wants to listen. When my grandfather finishes his pasta, he stands up slowly from the table and walks into the living room. He sits down in his favourite chair, a green Lazy Boy that he and my grandmother bought for half price at Honest Ed's Midnight Madness Extravaganza thirty-two years ago.

I walk over to see if my grandfather is all right. He has his eyes shut, but I can tell he is not sleeping.

"Can I get you anything?" I ask.

"No," he says. "I just need to rest."

I watch as my grandfather picks up a picture from the table next to his chair. It is a black and white photo in an old hand-carved frame. The photo is of a young man sitting awkwardly on a cheap wooden chair. I know which picture it is without looking at it.

"I had beautiful hair then," he says, and slowly puts the picture back on the table. He reaches for the remote and turns on the television. He leans back in the Lazy Boy and pretends to sleep. His bald head looks very small against the back of the chair.

TO DANCE
THE BEGINNING OF THE WORLD

I[1] won Columbus the goldfish accidently at the Richmond Hill Spring Fair in the summer of 1972. In itself, this may not seem like such a notewothy event,[2] but it happened during the great date of my life.[3] There is nothing which can ruin a date more effectively than a goldfish.[4]

My name is Brian Canham, and I was once a sixteen-year-old virgin. I remember days when I felt like I was the only person on the

---

[1] Of course, I am no longer the insecure teenager I once was, but I refuse to play the complicated post-modern games that so many writers love to engage in. This is not a riddle of delayed signification, it is a pure story; the story of how I lost my virginity.

[2] A goldfish life consists of swimming, eating, and defecating. Nothing remarkable ever happens. Even the death of a goldfish occurs without much fanfare. You wake up one morning to discover that the goldfish is not swimming as well as it did the day before. The next morning you find that it is unable to do anything other than float listlessly at the top of the bowl. Then suddenly — almost as if it intends to catch you by surprise — it splashes violently around in the bowl. These are its death throes. And this is the moment when it is most alive. The fish understands nothing except that it does not want to die. It dies anyway. When it finally stops moving, you flush it down the toilet. Human beings treat each other in much the same way. When my wife (now my ex) called to say she was leaving me, I put the phone down very slowly and cried for the first time in fifteen years. I felt like the inside of a goldfish bowl.

[3] Of course, now that I can consider my life maturely as a whole, I can see that it was not the great date of my life, but only one of the great dates of my life. I like to think that the great date of my life is still ahead of me. I am only thirty-five, and this is something which I need to believe.

[4] With the possible exception of herpes. There is absolutely nothing which ruins a date more than realizing the other person has herpes. This has never actually happened to me, but I can imagine what it would be like. The closest I have ever come was in grade thirteen, when Norma Fullerstein informed me she had mono after we'd kissed.

planet who had not done it yet.[5] I am now seventeen, and of course, I have done it many times, but I can still remember what it was like never to have done it.

Our school expert on doing it is Peter Campbell. Peter is a tall blond guy who is captain of the basketball team. Peter goes out with Trish, a girl with huge dark eyes. She plays clarinet in the school band and comes to every basketball game.[6] Although she is the best-looking girl in the school, Peter cheats on her all the time. It seems like Peter is always doing it, and that when he is not actually doing it, he is thinking about new ways of doing it, or new people to do it with.

It was Peter who first gave me the idea to ask Diane out. We were warming up for a game when Peter dribbled over to me and pointed out Diane Vitesse in the stands.

"Do you know her?" he asked.

"Sure," I replied. "Why?"

"She thinks you're cute."

---

[5] Every period has its own euphemism for sex: boff, boink, bop, bang, hump, fuck, do the dirty deed, ride the lizard, play hide the sausage, coitus, laying pipe, the old in-out, schtupping, slapping bellies, tonsil hockey, hanging the chandelier, frisking the pony, making the beast with two backs, the hot and sloppy, getting down and dirty, getting it on, getting it, doing it, plugging it — the list goes on and on, but it all means the same thing. In Elizabethan times, they called it, among other things, "to dance the beginning of the world." I think they knew what they were talking about: sex is the beginning and the end of the world; it is what really counts in the universe. My wife (now my ex) tells me her new lover is a young artist. I don't want to know what he looks like.

[6] However, while she came to all the games, she never came at any of the games. This sort of thing does not happen in high school, or at least didn't at my high school — it was in the suburbs. It was not until I was in university, when I met an Italian girl named Florence Berlini, that I had sex in a public place. We dated for about two months, but broke up because I couldn't take it any more. We would do it everywhere. On elevators, in public washrooms, in movie theatres, in cloakrooms, in closets and on buses. But she would never let me actually sleep with her. Sex in bed was boring, she said. Maria (my ex) used to hate it when I talked about Florence. Sometimes it is hard to remember that we aren't married anymore. I still can't sleep on her side of the bed.

"How do you know?"

"Trish told me."

"What did she say?"

"Trish said that the other day when they were in geography and Mr. Conway left the room they each wrote out lists of who they thought were the best-looking guys, and you were number two on her list."

"Really? Who was number one?"

"I was . . . but that doesn't matter — she would never do it with me."

"Why?"

"Because I'm not the right kind of guy. You are. Diane is just waiting for the right kind of guy to do it with. She hasn't done it yet, but she will.

"So what should I do?"

"Ask her out," he said simply, and dribbled away.

During the game, each time I got a basket, I would look up at Diane in the stands, to see her reaction. Once — after a turnaround jumpshot from just behind the foul line — I looked up into the stands, and she waved at me.[7]

Peter was right, she did think I was cute. Tomorrow, before math class, I would ask her out.[8]

---

[7] In high school, a wave is a definite indication of love. Girls in high school don't just wave at anybody. And this was no ordinary wave; it was a wave with weight. It is only in later life, after sour love affairs and selfish people have calloused one's heart, that a wave becomes insignificant. A wave — in high school — is not unlike a phone call late in the night, during which the person on the other end of the line doesn't say a word, but nevertheless communicates, by simply breathing, their name and that they think they cannot live without you.

[8] At the time, it seemed as if everything in my life had been transformed. When the game was over, I ran all the way home, and helped my sister set the table. After dinner, I kissed my mother on the cheek and told her that the meal was delicious. My father came up to my room later in the evening and asked me if I was taking drugs. I explained that I was in love.

"Don't tell your mother," he said quickly, and closed the door behind him.

The next day, I got to math class early, right after lunch. Diane always arrived a little early for class, so it was no problem knowing where to find her. The math teacher had not yet opened the door, and when I got there she was standing outside the classroom, alone.

I knew that if I hesitated I would chicken out, so I just took a deep breath, walked up to her, and started talking.[9]

"Hi Diane," I said. "How are you?"

"Fine," she replied.

"Fine," I said, not realizing that she had not asked me, then added, "You're looking nice today."

"Why, thank you," she answered. For a moment we looked at each other in silence. I looked at my shoes, and Diane lightly shook her pencil case.

Then she broke the silence.

"You played a really good game yesterday."

"Thanks."

For a moment we just looked at each other. She scratched behind her ear; I took a deep breath. Then we both laughed.

"Do you want to go out Friday?" I said suddenly.

"Like on a date?"

Holding my breath, I nodded.

She looked away, at the math book in her hands, and said, "I guess."

"Really?" I exclaimed, finally exhaling.

"Sure, why not?" she asked.

"I don't know."

"You don't know what?"

"I don't know why not."

"Neither do I," she said

---

[9] Asking her was like jumping into a swimming pool. I felt like I was standing on a diving board and looking into the cold water beneath me. When you dive into a pool there is always that moment — when you are suspended in mid-air — when you wonder what ever made you want to get wet in the first place.

"So then, it's OK?" I said to be sure.

"It's OK," she said, with finality.

Then we both laughed.[10]

"When do you want to meet?" she asked.

"Eight?"

"Sure," she said. "Maybe we could go to the fair."

"Good idea."

I can't recall anything about math class that day other than the discovery that by turning my head in a certain way, I could look at Diane and the math teacher at the same time.

I wondered what it would be like to kiss her. Was I really in love?[11] I wondered what she was thinking. I wondered if she was thinking about me. I started to think about what our date would be like. I would walk over to her house and pick her up around eight. Then we would take the bus to the fair. We would go on some rides, get something to eat, and then I would walk her home. Then what would happen? I wondered if she liked me enough to do it. Soon, I was thinking about actually doing it.

That was when I began to get nervous.

Really nervous.

In fact, I started to panic. I considered telling her after school that I couldn't make it that night. I could say that I had just remembered a family commitment, or that I had to take my brother to the doctor. I could get someone else to go with her. I could ask Peter. She

---

10 It has been said that there is comfort in knowing that you are damned, but there is damn more comfort in knowing that you have a date.

11 This was a much easier question then — when I had never been in love before — than it is today. At sixteen love seemed like a great adventure. Today I don't even know what love is. Six months ago, when Maria and I spoke for the last time, I started to cry again. On the phone, she seemed like a different person. I asked what I had done to deserve this.

"It wasn't your fault," she told me. "Stop torturing yourself."

"Then why?" I asked. "Why did it have to happen?"

"People change," she said, and hung up the phone.

thought he was cuter than me anyway. I could just not show up. But then she would tell her friends and I would never get a date for the rest of my life. I could call her that night and say that I had come down with the flu, but then I would have to stay at home and my parents would think I was taking drugs. There seemed to be no way out.

When the class ended, I ran out of the classroom as fast as I could, not even looking at Diane. By the time I walked into basketball practice after school I was a nervous wreck.

"What's the matter with you?" asked Peter, as we changed into our gym clothes.

"I just asked Diane out," I told him shakily.

"Really," he said. "Where are you going?"

"To the fair."

"Right on!" he said, shaking his fist the same way he does when someone on the team scores a foul shot.

"Hey, everybody," he called out to the change room in general, "Brian has a date with Diane."

"Right on," everyone called back, shaking their fists.

John Pesner, the center on the team, walked over to me. I thought he was going to shake my hand, but he didn't. Instead, he pressed a little plastic package in my palm.

"Don't forget to put your boots on," he said.

I looked at the white package and smiled weakly.

"You're not shooting blanks anymore," he reminded me, as the changeroom suddenly became very quiet.

Putting the condom between my teeth, I bent down to tie my shoes. "Yeah," I said weakly, trying my best to mean it, "I know what I'm doing. She's just waiting for the right guy."

"Right on," said an unfamiliar deep voice. It was Mr. Williams, the basketball coach. He was making the fist.[12]

---

[12] Mr. Williams was so politically incorrect that he was politically uncorrect. Even his grammar was offensive.

At the fair the air smelled of grass cuttings, gasoline, cigarettes and candy floss. Diane was wearing a white dress and high heels. With her heels on, she was about two inches taller than me. She looked very different than at school, where she wore jeans most of the time. I didn't comment on it, however, figuring that she was thinking the same thing about me. I was wearing ripped jeans, a black Van Halen t-shirt, white Reebox shoes, and Aqua Velva aftershave.[13]

"What do you want to do first?" I asked as we walked toward the entrance.

"It's up to you," she said cheerfully, and began to hold my hand.

I didn't want to go on rides yet, and it was too early to get anything to eat, so I suggested that we play some of the games.

"That looks like fun." Diane pointed at a booth where a huge red bear was hanging. Underneath the bear was a multicoloured pyramid of goldfish bowls.

"Let's give it a try," I said.

"What do you do?" I asked the guy who ran the stand.

"It's easy," he told me. "You throw the ball, and if it lands in the bowl filled with red water, you get the bear. If it lands in one of the other bowls you get another prize. As long as you get it in a bowl, you get a prize. Everyone's a winner."

It really didn't look that difficult. There was only one bowl with red water, and it was at the top. You either got the ball right into it, or missed completely. I got three balls for a dollar.

My first try missed the pyramid of bowls completely.[14] I threw the ball straight at the red bowl as hard as I could. I wanted to put it straight in. The ball did not even touch any of the bowls. It was very embarrassing.

---

[13] I was dressed to kill.

[14] Your first try at anything is always painful to remember. Anything you have never tried seems easy. Other people might tell you that it is difficult, but until you give it a shot yourself, you never believe them. My throw at the red bowl was

I threw the next ball on a wide arch, aiming as closely as possible at the red bowl.[15] But again, I missed all of the bowls.

"Good throw," said Diane, and kissed me softly on the cheek. "That was for good luck," she told me when I looked at her, surprised.

---

so optimistic it was painful. I thought that I could win the prize with one magical throw. It reminds me of Cynthia Lefcoe, the first woman I ever really loved. We met at the University of Guelph. Cynthia sat next to me in ENG 332Y. One day I borrowed a pen from her and asked if she would like to see a movie that night. She had long red hair, and spoke in a soft voice that never seemed able to raise itself above an insistent whisper. Like me, she would be graduating that spring. We went on a few dates, and then, even before we realized what was happening, we found ourselves in love. Some nights after we made love she would cry. I never asked her why. I knew that she was thinking about the future. Soon the letters of acceptance began to arrive. I got into the teaching program at the U of T, and she decided to do her graduate work at UBC. For the summer, we got a small apartment and moved in together. That summer was perfect. We didn't have to work, we didn't have to think; life was uncomplicated.

Eventually, September came and we had to go our separate ways. We wrote long letters to each other, and there were a few tearful long-distance phone calls, but soon we drifted apart. Today Cynthia is the editor of a small literary magazine called *The Paper's Edge* and is married to a Vancouver lawyer.

I don't like to remember that summer. She was going to be a poet, and I was going to be The Great Canadian Novelist. "I'll be a high-school teacher only for a little while," I told her.

We promised each other that after we got our degrees and made some money we would move to Paris and live in squalor, just like Henry and June. Our love was like any first try; it was full of self-confidence, hope, and folly.

[15] My second try was different because I thought I knew what I was doing. It was like when I met my wife. I had just graduated from teachers college. I was teaching grade nine English at Bathurst Heights High School. I had a good salary, but was still living in the same small, cheap apartment that I had occupied as a student. Two years had passed since my breakup with Cynthia. One weekend, an old friend called and invited me to go on a double date with him. I didn't want to go, but he insisted. My date that night was a petite, dark woman named Maria Perry (now my ex). During the date, the other couple got into a fight and went home early. Neither Maria nor I wanted to be alone on a Friday, so we went out for coffee. At the time, she was working in a small art supply store, but she wanted to be a publicist. She was making some good contacts, and was hoping to go into business for herself. A week later we went out again, and in a year we were

I took my last ping-pong ball into my hand,[16] and decided to trust the winds of chance.

I closed my eyes and threw the ball straight up, in the general direction of the pyramid of fishbowls. It fell into one of the bowls filled with green water and a fish.

"We got a winner!" announced the man who ran the game.

---

married. When I was offered a better paying job in the suburbs just north of Toronto, we moved out of my apartment and bought a house. We lived there for seven years.

Those were very good years. I settled into my job and Maria was having increasing success as a publicist. I even finished a few chapters of the novel I had always said I would write. It would be called called *The Quiet Painter*. The painter is very poor, but the small room in which he sleeps, eats, and paints does not bother him. His friends — men who have become doctors, lawyers, and teachers — try to convince him to take a more practical approach to life. He refuses, and goes on painting. One day he meets a slim dancer with auburn hair and falls in love with her. She is more beautiful than any woman he has ever imagined. At first, he cannot bring himself even to touch her. But when he does, a terrible thing happens. He thinks that something has happened to his fingers. It seems as if his hands have a mind of their own. Soon it is apparent that he has become obsessed with her, and he cannot paint anything but portraits of her.

That was as far as I got. At the time, I didn't know how to end it. I didn't have anything left to say.

The years I spent with Maria were very good. We loved our jobs, we loved our life, and we loved each other. But one day it all ended. Maria began to spend more time at the gallery. She never answered any of my questions. I was angry and confused and hurt. I didn't know what was happening. I felt betrayed. Then one night, the phone rang, and Maria informed me that she would not be coming home. She would drop by next week to pick up her things. She was in love with someone else. She was filing for divorce. I got the papers in the mail. Even when you think you understand the way things work, your second try is little better than your first.

[16] I could pay a dollar and try again, but then it might seem like I was trying too hard to win. The most important thing about winning is not looking like you care. I just closed my eyes and threw the last ball into the air because I understood that there was nothing I could do that would make any difference. If something is going to happen, it will happen, regardless of anything we do. One person cannot choose to stop loving another person any more than a star can decide to become a supernova. The secret is knowing when to close your eyes.

"You won!" Diane yelled.

"A winner! A winner! A winner!" screamed the carnie again, this time into a megaphone. People walking by looked at me and smiled. Then he handed me my prize in a dirty plastic bag. It was a goldfish.

"See you later," said the man. "Have a good time with the fish."

I handed Diane the bag to look at.

"What a cute little guy," she said.

"But you wanted the bear . . ."

"No, I didn't want the bear. Anybody could have won me the bear, but the goldfish is something special."[17]

---

[17] I had no idea that she really wanted a goldfish, but it was the thing that made Diane fall instantly in love with me. It is amazing the way things work out sometimes. Diane and I dated for about a year, but had to break up when her family moved to Florida. I have not seen her since. I wonder sometimes what she looks like today.

It has been almost a year since Maria called to tell me that she was not coming back, and I am beginning to get used to the idea.

I have even started to write again, and my novel is almost finished. The beautiful dancer leaves the painter, but he goes on painting her anyway. Near the end he becomes very ill, and the woman comes to visit him one last time before he dies. She is amazed to discover that the walls of his little room are covered with magnificent portraits of herself. Instantly, she falls back in love with him. He is too weak to say anything. Against his wishes, she invites a woman who is a publicist from a prestigious downtown gallery to see the room. The publicist is equally impressed, and begins to arrange a huge exhibition. The painter dies tragically, before the exhibition opens, in the arms of the woman he has always loved and whose portraits surround them. The last image in the novel is of his fingers touching her lips, one last time, before they go cold forever.

It isn't realistic, and it's far too predictable to be serious literature, but I like it. It's exactly the kind of book that I wanted to write. It's not about the way that things really are, but the way they should be. No one wants realism anyway. People want a happy ending; they need to dream. Realism is for short stories like this — things you can forget easily.

Next week, I am supposed to start ballroom dancing lessons with an oriental woman who teaches at the same school as I do. Her husband died of lung cancer two years ago. It is amazing the way people are able to bounce back. We are the tennis balls of the stars; they are too distant to understand how their games seem to us. We are goldfish of a different sort.

Then she kissed me again, on the lips.

"Let's name him Columbus," suggested Diane. "He looks kind of like an explorer, doesn't he?"

"Actually, he does."

"This is turning out to be quite the little adventure," she said, and kissed me on the lips again. This time she stuck her tongue into my mouth.

"Do you have so much fun every time you go out?" I asked.

"Not every time," she replied smiling. "I guess you're just the right kind of guy."

Later that night we sat on a bench at Don Head Park, just behind her house and kissed each other carefully. Then we lay down in the grass.

Perched on the edge of the park bench, Columbus seemed oblivious to what we were doing. At Diane's house we put him into a pickle jar, and he looked happy. We were very quiet, so that we wouldn't wake up her parents, and she kissed me once more before I left. On my way home I stopped a couple of times and laid down on the grass to look at the stars. My underwear was wet on the inside, and I realized that a little bit of my life had just happened.

THE SWEET SECOND KISS
OF FLORENCE FERGUSON

for Matt Cohen

Herbert Luckett fell in love with Florence Ferguson on April 11, 1980. It happened in front of Richmond Hill High School. The school day had just ended. They were both seventeen years old and standing under the same umbrella.

"My mother is coming to get me," Florence told Herbert. "She can give you a ride home if you want. We're going your way — she's taking me out to buy shoelaces."

It is perhaps because Herbert Luckett has become head of the English department at Richmond Hill High School that he still remembers that day with such clarity. He is not obsessed with the memory, but neither is it uncommon — on certain April afternoons — for the image of the seventeen-year-old Florence Ferguson to impinge on his consciousness.

On these days he knows he must be careful.

He must be careful not to walk into any solid objects. He must be careful not to skip any of the classes he is supposed to teach. He must be careful to remind himself — upon passing heads of red hair that smell a certain way, or after hearing the letter S pronounced in a distinctive manner — that Florence Ferguson graduated from Richmond Hill High School almost twenty years ago.

It is on such days that Herbert Luckett quietly retires to his office and pretends to read. He sits in his chair with a book open in front of him, and his eyes move, but only his body is reading. His mind is elsewhere. His mind is standing beside Florence Ferguson in the rain.

In these private reconstructions of that afternoon, Herbert Luckett has decided there were five reasons for his falling in love with Florence Ferguson:

1) The smell of Florence's hair. Herbert tells himself that the fragrance was like "roses in the rain." (It was produced by a mixture of Finesse Shampoo, Secret Under Arm Deodorant, Babe Perfume (a now-discontinued product of Shoppers Drug Mart), Alberto Medium Hold Hairspray, and the egg-salad sandwich she had eaten for lunch that day.)

2) Florence's articulation of the word "shoelaces." Her pronunciation was not completely flawless. Florence placed a slight lisp on the second S that made Herbert think, momentarily, that she was about to begin whistling *Sweet Georgia Brown*. (A piece of music that Florence and Herbert collectively identified as *The Globetrotter Theme*.)

3) The Umbrella. Florence tilted the umbrella slightly so the excess water from the top of it would run onto herself and not onto Herbert. Herbert has often reflected that holding an umbrella in such a manner is the purest gesture of selflessness one human being can make to another. (Florence held the umbrella that way because her hand was tired.)

4) The stars were right. Herbert has always secretly believed there was some kind of cosmic power exerting its force on him that day. (He is not completely wrong. However, it was not the stars that were "right." It was the planet Mars. At the moment Florence was saying the word "shoelaces" the planet Mars drifted into the constellation Cassiopeia, an event which had a marked effect on all men born on January 13, 1963 between 2:28 pm and 3:01 pm.)

5) The rain. Herbert has always contended that one is more likely to fall in love when it is raining. Herbert's falling in love manifested itself through a series of barely perceptible physical changes. First his cheeks became slightly flushed. Then his eyes glazed over. Then he began to feel taller. It is a largely overlooked fact that whenever anyone falls in love, they immediately begin to feel taller. The history of the world is

the history of people who stand next to other people in the rain, discover they are feeling taller, and like it that way. This is what happened to Herbert Luckett. On that April afternoon, he was five foot eight, but after Florence Ferguson said the word "shoelaces," he felt as if he were at least five foot eleven.

However, Herbert was unaware that he had just fallen in love. This was primarily because he was beginning to get an erection and secondarily because, as a seventeen-year-old boy, he did not think in terms of falling in, or out, of love. Instead, he looked at Florence and told himself she was "hot".

Florence was not thinking of love either.

She was thinking of shoelaces.

More precisely, she was contemplating her shoes — a pair of black and white saddle shoes with extremely frayed black laces — and was debating what sort of replacement shoelaces would suit her best. She had already ruled out the possibility of crazy shoelaces, the kind with candy canes, or small dwarves on them. Black laces were the obvious choice. However, the last thing that Florence wanted to be was obvious. White shoelaces would be certain to create a stir in the decidedly conservative fashion community of Richmond Hill High School, but Florence also had certain misgivings about taking such a pioneering and possibly trend-setting step. She was about to put the question to Herbert when her mother's lime-green Gremlin pulled up in front of the school.

"Hello, Herbert," said Mrs. Ferguson, who turned around in her seat and smiled at him as he was getting into the back seat.

"Hello, Mrs. Ferguson," he replied, smiling back at her.

"I said we could give Herbert a ride home, seeing as we're going his way," Florence told her mother.

"That will be fine," said Mrs. Ferguson, who turned around in her seat and smiled again at Herbert.

Herbert smiled back at her, again.

Such a quiet boy, thought Mrs. Ferguson, and so well mannered. He's much thinner than his father. "You live on Mill Street, don't you?" she asked him.

"It's near the pond," Florence told her mother before Herbert could say anything. "I'll show you which house."

Although Florence had never seen the inside of the Luckett house, she knew exactly where it was. She possessed this information as a result of attending Lisa Mollet's birthday party in the seventh grade. When that party was over Lisa's mother drove everyone home. They were driving down Mill Street when Lisa Mollet pointed out the window and whispered, "That's where Herbert Luckett lives" to Florence. Florence looked out of the window and saw the orange bricks and the basketball net, and then looked at Lisa and nodded without comment. It was a well-documented fact that Lisa Mollet had always had a huge crush on Herbert Luckett. At the time, Florence was firm in the conviction that boys were disgusting.

The three of them drove down Mill Street in silence. Mrs. Ferguson was driving, but thinking about Herbert. Herbert was thinking about Florence. Florence was thinking about shoelaces.

"I think I'll get white shoelaces," said Florence decisively.

"Whatever you want," said Mrs. Ferguson. "They're your laces."

"Do you think I should get white shoelaces?" Florence asked Herbert. "Remember they're for black and white saddle shoes," she added.

"I guess," replied Herbert.

Florence nodded to herself and looked out the window. "We're coming up to it," she said, and pointed to Herbert's house.

Mrs. Ferguson pulled into the Luckett driveway.

"Thanks," said Herbert, and got out of the car. He closed the door and looked at Florence one last time before walking up the front steps of his house.

"He seems like a nice boy," said Mrs. Ferguson. "Quite handsome, really."

That was when Florence looked at her mother, and then sat up slightly straighter in her seat.

To The Casual Observer, unschooled in the subtle nuances of the Ferguson clan, nothing would have seemed out of the ordinary.

The Casual Observer would have looked through the back windshield and seen a mother and a daughter having a harmless and profoundly mundane conversation about the boy who had just then got out of the car.

The Casual Observer would not have noticed the way Mrs. Ferguson blinked three times after saying the word "handsome."

The Casual Observer would not have grasped the significance of the slight blush that rose to the cheeks of Mrs. Ferguson after she blinked three times.

The Casual Observer would not have thought there was anything unusual about the soft, almost girlish giggle which Mrs. Ferguson could not prevent escaping from her lips after the slight blush rose to her cheeks.

However, Florence Ferguson was No Casual Observer.

Florence looked at her mother and knew, knew with a certainty that can only belong to a daughter, that her mother wanted Herbert Luckett.

This was the idea that made Florence sit up slightly straighter in her seat.

Until that moment, Florence had never imagined her mother wanting anyone. Like most people between the ages of eight and thirty-two, Florence thought of her mother as a good-natured, but deeply flawed approximation of a human being. For that reason, Florence did not attribute to her certain characteristics that are commonly thought of as belonging to normal human beings. One of these characteristics was lust. Until that April afternoon, Florence had never imagined her mother possessed the ability to lust.

It was the idea of her mother wanting Herbert Luckett that made Florence take a second look at him. She watched him climb the front steps of his house, and — for the first time — perceived him as a sexual being. However, she did not articulate this revelation to herself in just this way. Instead, she formulated her new awareness in terms that are typical of, and perhaps confined to, High School Girls Who Have Yet To Be Kissed. "I guess he's kinda cute," Florence told her mother.

Mrs. Ferguson nodded and pulled out of the Luckett driveway. She drove down Mill Street in the direction of the shoe store. Florence bought white shoelaces, and by the time they got home it had stopped raining.

It was her recently acquired perception of Herbert Luckett as a sexual being which kept Florence Ferguson from immediately discarding the note that was placed on her grade twelve English class desk the next day. The note was sealed in a white envelope and her name was written neatly, in black ink, on the front of it. After looking quickly around the classroom to make sure no one was watching, Florence opened the letter. It read:

> *Dear Florence,*
>   *Do you*
>   *a) want to go to a movie tonight?*
>   *b) like carrots?*
>   *c) want me to get lost?*
>   *d) none of the above (fill in your own)*
>
> *Yours,*
>   *Herbert Luckett*

Florence put the note down and looked across the room at Herbert, who was looking back at her and beaming. It was not a smile. It was more than a smile. It was a movement with his mouth that made it look like he wanted to reach behind his lips, tear out his teeth, and fling them across the room to Florence as a token of his affection.

Florence looked at Herbert and his straight brown hair that was parted straight down the middle of his head, and wondered what her mother saw in him. Florence was not overly impressed with the letter, but she did not throw it into the garbage. Neither did she turn him down immediately.

Florence folded the letter and put it into the back pocket of her jeans. And then she turned her full attention to the lesson being taught. She did this despite Herbert's insistent stare, which never wavered once from her face for the duration of the class, except briefly, when he was called on by the teacher to provide the name of the country in which Hamlet lived and to give his impression of the weather in that part of the world.

When the class ended, Florence exited the classroom without even glancing at Herbert.

Florence was kneeling in front of her locker and trying to locate her math book when Herbert caught up to her.

"Did you get the letter?" he asked.

"I got it," replied Florence. "You saw me open it." She had just discovered her math book pressed against the rotten banana that resided permanently at the bottom of her locker. She wiped the banana off and stood up to face Herbert.

'Well?" he asked.

"Well what?" she asked him back.

"Well, I mean — I saw you read the letter. Do you want to go to a movie tomorrow?"

"I don't know," said Florence. "I haven't made up my mind yet."

For a moment Herbert didn't know what to say. He cracked the knuckles on his right hand. Florence looked at him with distaste and he did not crack the other hand.

"I'll let you know," said Florence finally.

"Great," said Herbert, despite his disappointment.

"I've got to get to class," said Florence.

The two of them then walked in an easterly direction, toward room 178, neither of them knowing that Herbert was about to utter the eleven words that would make the heart of the beautiful, but chaste, Florence Ferguson melt.

"I like those jeans," said Herbert. "They're the same colour as your eyes."

Florence laughed and kept walking. She said something about her mother putting too much bleach in the wash and pretended to ignore the compliment.

But the moment she said goodbye to Herbert, she walked straight to the girls' bathroom and stood in front of the mirror.

Florence Ferguson turned thirty-seven last February.

She is married to Colin Sherbick, of Sherbick, Stong, and Lawlor Barristers and Solicitors. They have three children. They live in a large house in Forest Hill.

If you ask her about falling in love, she will tell you one of two stories.

She may tell you the story of how she and Colin met at the University of Toronto when they were both undergraduates. It happened in the Robarts Library. They were reaching for the same volume of Whitman when their hands touched. If Florence has had a couple of drinks, she will insist that the moment their fingertips intersected, she felt a strong electrical charge shake her entire body. She will tell you that was the moment she knew she wanted to marry Colin.

However, if she is in a different mood (and has not had a couple of drinks) Florence will tell you the other story: the story of how Colin proposed to her. It was in Boston. Colin was studying law at Harvard at the time. They had just finished dinner at *Le Coq* and were walking down by the river when — completely out of the blue — Colin got down on his knees and proposed to her. Strangers walking by stopped to look. When Florence accepted, they cheered. Florence will tell you she looked at Colin kneeling on the sidewalk and knew she wanted to spend the rest of her life with him.

Herbert Luckett has three daughters (the youngest is named Florence) and is married to a woman named Christine whom he met at the University of Guelph when they were both in the teaching program there. She is a kindergarten teacher. She does not have red hair. They have a good life together. Aside from certain April afternoons when Herbert is seized by Memory in the hallways of Richmond Hill High School, he does not think of Florence Ferguson that often.

He has only seen Florence once in the last twenty years. She looked older and had put on some weight, but she still had the same red hair. He knew it was her immediately.

He saw her at the SuperCentre in Richmond Hill. Herbert was pushing a shopping cart with two children in it. He was going to say hello to her, but decided against it. Florence looked absorbed in her own thoughts. She was holding two loaves of bread in her hands and looking into space. Herbert wondered if perhaps she was having some kind of family trouble, if her mother was sick, or if her marriage was collapsing. He saw the look of concentration on Florence's face and decided not to say anything.

Florence was trying to decide between white bread and brown bread.

She finally settled on the white bread and went to pay for her groceries. She pushed her shopping cart right past Herbert Luckett and his two small children without giving him a second look.

On the way home from the supermarket, Herbert tried to tell himself Florence did not recognize him because he had lost most of his hair and had put on twenty pounds. He tried to tell himself she was preoccupied with more important things. He tried to tell himself that he really didn't care whether or not Florence Ferguson knew who he was or not.

His wife was making roast beef for dinner. They went out to a movie that night. When they got home, Herbert drove the babysitter home. His wife said she was exhausted and went straight to bed. Herbert stayed up late to watch Letterman. That was Friday. By Sunday, he had stopped thinking about having seen Florence Ferguson at the SuperCentre.

Herbert Luckett and Florence Ferguson never had what can properly be called a love affair. They went out on a couple of dates and they kissed more than once, but that was the extent of their relationship. They were never really going out. They never thought about getting engaged. She never wanted him.

But of course, they have not forgotten each other. Complete forgetfulness is a fiction. Florence will tell you her two romantic stories about Colin, and Herbert will go on about his three beautiful daughters; but nothing that either of them tell you will have anything to do with the truth.

The truth is that the first time Florence Ferguson fell in love with anyone was when she stood in the Richmond Hill High School bathroom on April 12, 1980 and saw that Herbert was right. Her jeans were the same colour as her eyes.

That day, she went to her math class and tried to pretend nothing had happened. However, for every 8 she had to write that day, she wrote an H instead. When the class was finished, she got out the note, circled the letter A and wrote "pick me up at seven" beside it. Then she re-folded the note and slipped it into the bottom of Herbert's locker.

After the movie, Florence Ferguson and Herbert Luckett sat in his father's turquoise Pontiac Parisian and looked at each other.

Neither of them said anything for what seemed like a long time. Florence cleared her throat and then smiled. Herbert got a very serious look on his face. Then he leaned toward her. And they kissed.

It was not a great kiss. It was a first kiss. It was a kiss that Florence had to get out of the way before moving on, later in her life, to increasingly complicated, longer, and more accurate kisses (Herbert positioned his mouth slightly too far to the left and, as a result, dampened Florence's right cheek). However, for a first kiss, it was greatly improved by Florence's beginning to emit a low-pitched purring sound that not even she, in her most private moments, had ever heard before. Herbert took this to mean he was doing something right, and so, almost before The First Kiss of Florence Ferguson had ended, he embarked upon the second.

The Sweet Second Kiss of Florence Ferguson was still in its infancy when, fearing scandal, gossip, pregnancy, hell, and her father, Florence announced she "had to go" and got out of the car.

Herbert told her goodbye, but did not drive away until he was sure Florence's skirted knees made it safely through the front door of her house.

In the Ferguson house, her father was the only one awake. He was watching television. Florence told him she was home and then went upstairs. She got into bed with all her clothes on and without brushing her teeth.

This book was typeset
in stylized Palatino, Georgia, Times
and Zapfdingbats fonts.